KU-265-205

CRIMEA

Michael Pope,
110th Regiment, 1853-1857

by Bryan Perrett

SCHOLASTIC

While the events described and some of the characters in this book may be based on actual historical events and real people, Michael Pope is a fictional character, created by the author, and his story is a work of fiction.

Scholastic Children's Books
Commonwealth House, 1–19 New Oxford Street,
London, WC1A 1NU, UK
A division of Scholastic Ltd
London ~ New York ~ Toronto ~ Sydney ~ Auckland
Mexico City ~ New Delhi ~ Hong Kong

Published in the UK by Scholastic Ltd, 2002

Copyright © Bryan Perrett, 2002

All rights reserved

ISBN 0 439 98111 5

Typeset by Falcon Oast Graphic Art Ltd, East Hoathly, East Sussex
Printed and bound in Great Britain by Mackays of Chatham Limited, Chatham, Kent
Cover image: Detail from Trumpeter Critten, Trumpeter Lang – Royal Artillery,
1856. The Royal Archives © Her Majesty Queen Elizabeth II/J Cundall and R Howlett
Background image: Detail from Soldiers of the 86th Regiment skirmishing.
Courtesy of the Director, National Army Museum, London.

2 4 6 8 10 9 7 5 3 1

The right of Bryan Perrett to be identified as the author of this work has been asserted by him in accordance with the Copyright, Designs and Patents Act, 1988.

This book is sold subject to the condition that it shall not, by way of trade or otherwise be lent, resold, hired out, or otherwise circulated without the publisher's prior consent in any form of binding or cover other than that in which it is published and without a similar condition, including this condition, being imposed upon the subsequent purchaser.

1857

My name is Michael Pope and I was born in the year 1839. I am the third oldest of my father's sons and I have four brothers and five sisters. For the past four years I have served as a drummer in Her Majesty's 110th Regiment of Foot. The story that I am about to tell you, my story, is about my adventures in the Crimean War, during which I took part in the storming of the Heights of Alma, witnessed the heroic Charge of the Light Brigade at Balaklava, and was present at the capture of the Russians' great fortress of Sevastopol. I shall begin by telling you how it was that I came to join the Army...

June 1853

My father was a wheelwright and a good one. Some said he was too good, for he was painstaking and thorough, so that it would be many years before a wheel he made or mended required attention. Indeed, because he worked so slowly he was not always able to accept all the business he was offered. It was difficult for him to put bread upon the table for us all, for although my two elder brothers helped him, his income was not sufficient to feed, clothe and house so large a family. It was different when my mother was alive, for when she was not suckling she taught reading and writing to the children of the village and the surrounding farms, and that brought in sufficient extra money for us to live modestly but without worry. Seeing that I inherited her love of music, she taught me to read that, too. Our little church was too poor to afford an organ for many a long year yet, so instead we had a band that played from the gallery at the back, and in this I began to play the cornet when I was twelve years of age. Sadly, my mother died while giving birth to the last of us. My father loved her dearly, as we all did, and the heart seemed to go out of him when she passed over. That, and the worry of supporting us, made him grow old before his time. My eldest sister, upon whom the burden of running our home descended, was betrothed to the son of a farmer. We missed her when they were wed, although, as my father commented, not unkindly, there was one less mouth to feed.

Our village, Feldon St Mary, was very small, although we were large enough to have our own cricket team. We had an old inn called the Saracen's Head, and also a Post Office that sold necessary items. For ought else we had to go to Thornbury, the county town, some five miles distant. The River Thorn winds round three sides of the hill on which the town is built. On top of the hill is a ruined castle and below that is the Cathedral. The rest of the town consists of narrow streets containing many shops. I was taken to Thornbury four or five times when I was younger. I remember the first time well, because it was the day the railway opened. I was eight years old at the time and was amazed by the bands and the flags and the crowd cheering when the first train arrived. I remember the engine was all gleaming brass and sparkling green paint, hissing steam and puffing smoke. After that, I thought that it would be a grand thing to work upon the railway. Indeed, during one visit to the town I went to the station and asked about the possibility of obtaining work there. I thought the wages I would bring in would help the family, but I was told that I was too young and that anyway there were no vacancies, all jobs being highly prized and much sought after. I was also told that I would be better off looking for a job in one of the manufactories springing up in the towns, because they paid better wages than could be had in the country.

In the summer of 1853 I turned fourteen years of age. One day in June I was sweeping out our workshop when I heard the approaching beat of a drum. Little of interest happens in Feldon St Mary and I loved a band, so I ran out into the road, followed by my older brothers, William and Fred. Everyone else was coming out of their houses to watch a file of a dozen soldiers entering the village. As they did so the beat of the drum changed and two of the soldiers with fifes struck up a tune I knew as "O'er the Hills and Far Away".

The drummer and the fifers wore white coats and the rest of the soldiers scarlet. There were half a dozen men in civilian clothes, too, trying to march like the soldiers but not doing very well, and I imagined that they were new recruits. The party halted at the Saracen's Head and were soon settled on the benches outside, enjoying the hot summer sun while the sergeant ordered ale for everyone, including most of us village lads, who had joined the curious crowd around the soldiers. When everyone was served, the sergeant commanding the party stood on one of the benches. He was an imposing figure with a straight back and a well-trimmed beard and moustache. On his tunic two medals were pinned. One, with a blue and red ribbon, had bars across it saying ALIWAL and SOBRAON; the other, with a blue and gold ribbon, had bars saying MOOLTAN and GOOJERAT. The words did not mean anything to me at the time, although I thought that they must be the names of battles in which the sergeant had taken part. The crowd fell silent as he started to speak.

"I am Sergeant Thomas Hancock and I am proud to belong to the 110th Regiment of Foot, the finest in Her Majesty's Army," he said in a commanding voice. "I'm a plain-speaking man and I won't beat about the bush. I'm here looking for a likely lad or two to join our ranks. I'm not looking for mother's boys or weaklings, and I'll only take the best you have to offer because soldiering is man's work."

For a moment there was silence, then my brother Fred asked him why anyone should want to go for a soldier when we were not at war.

"Well, that's a fair question," said Sergeant Hancock. "You remember that tune we played when we marched in? It's called 'O'er the Hills and Far Away', isn't it?" He pointed to a line of distant hills, blue and indistinct in the heat. "Now, can you tell me what's on the other side of those hills?"

Fred shook his head and said he'd never been that far from the village.

"No, and you won't find out either unless you get a move on!" replied the Sergeant, joining in the general laughter. "Now, what I say is this. A man will have nothing worthwhile to tell his children or his grandchildren unless he's been o'er the hills and seen what's beyond. That's where we'll take you and when you get back you'll have tales aplenty to tell of the sights you've seen and the things you've done. Like as not, you'll spend some time in India, where a soldier can live like a king. There'll be a char-wallah to bring

8

you tea in bed, a dhobi-wallah to do your washing, a punkah-wallah to fan the barrack room on hot nights, and more wallahs than you can think of to clean your boots and keep you spick and span, all for a few pence a week. What's more, you'll be paid regularly, you'll be given a smart uniform to wear and you'll be housed and fed at Her Majesty Queen Victoria's expense. And when your time is up, if you've kept out of trouble, you'll have a stripe or two on your arm and be given a pension – and still be young enough to work if you want to."

"I reckon all you'd be fit for is labouring," said Fred, keen to get his own back. "After all, the only thing a soldier knows is fighting."

"Ah, now that's where you're wrong," countered Sergeant Hancock. "There are plenty of employers who are happy to take on former non-commissioned officers because they know they'll be getting a man who is honest, straightforward, responsible and able to organize. As for myself, I'll be taking my discharge in three months' time and the London and North Western Railway Company have already offered me the post of station master on a new branch line they're to open shortly."

There was a murmur of approval from the crowd,

for a station master was a respected figure in any town and he was also well paid. It was at that moment I made up my mind, for if I went for a soldier there would be one less mouth for Father to feed and I might even be able to send him some of my pay to help him out. Better still, it seemed that I stood a good chance of being able to join one of the railway companies when my service was over.

"I'll join you," I said.

The crowd fell silent. Then Mrs Stringer, one of our neighbours, said, "You can't take him, Sergeant. He's only fourteen – and it's not two years since he lost his mother! Don't be such a young fool, Michael – you don't know what you're letting yourself in for."

For the moment my brothers were dumbfounded, but then William found his voice. "What d'you want to do that for? Time will come when Fred and I have learned the trade; we'll do more business and be able to pay you wages."

"Besides," added Fred, "you're only a nipper! You'll have to grow a bit afore you go fighting battles!"

"I can read and write," I said defiantly. "And I can read music and play the cornet. I can be a drummer boy."

The Sergeant stepped down, exchanging looks with

his corporal and drummer, who came across to look me over. Evidently satisfied, the three of them talked among themselves. Sergeant Hancock asked if my father was alive. I replied that he was and he said he would talk to him, telling the corporal to take the party on to Corunna Barracks in Thornbury, and that he hoped to follow shortly with me.

My father was horrified, saying at first that he would not permit me to join, for it was a disgrace for one of a family to go for a soldier, as it meant he was unfit for anything else and would be mixing with thieves and all manner of low persons. Why, he continued, had not the Duke of Wellington himself said that his army was composed of the scum of the earth?

"Ah, that may have been true before we got our hands on them, Mr Pope," rejoined Sergeant Hancock, quietly. "But you're forgetting the other half of the Duke's sentence, which was: 'it really is remarkable what fine fellows we have made of them.' If people took the trouble to talk to us, they would find us decent enough and not much different from them."

"It would be one less mouth for you to feed, Father," I said hopefully. The Sergeant was quick to take up the point, seeing immediately how short we were of money.

"Mr Pope," he said, "your son has asked to become a drummer, and when he is trained he will be paid at a better rate than a private soldier. Furthermore, because of his musical skills, I am authorized to pay him an immediate bounty of £5 once we all agree that he can be enlisted. He may wish to divide that sum with you, but that is a family matter and no concern of mine."

My father thought hard before finally reaching a decision. He said that the money was sorely needed, but it was up to me whether I went or not and he would not press me. I said I would go, at which Sergeant Hancock gave me £5 plus a day's pay when we had signed the paper. I gave the money to my father, who returned £2 to me, saying that it was a sad business and he wished it could be otherwise. My brothers and sisters, looking unhappy, said goodbye to me and wished me luck. My only possessions were the clothes I stood in, which had been handed down from my elder brothers, so there was nothing to pack. Emma, my favourite sister, who was aged eight, gave me a pencil and some paper, telling me to write. Then we were on our way. I felt a great sense of loss as I waved goodbye from the bend in the lane, but was excited, too, at the prospect of what lay ahead.

As we walked along the Thornbury road, Sergeant Hancock told me that I would not regret my decision, for a good regiment like the 110th was a family in itself and I would soon make good friends. He said that being a drummer was a responsible job, since in a battle it used to be the drummers who, by beating out the various calls, relayed the officers' orders. Nowadays, he said, the custom was dying out and it was the bugle that was more commonly used for such purposes.

"Does that mean I shall have to learn the bugle as well?" I asked.

"That you will," he replied. "But since you already play the cornet you'll have no difficulty. We still take our drums into action, and, what's more, in peacetime the Band and Drums are the smartest men in the regiment, always playing at shows and such, at which they are much admired by the ladies. Mind you, young Michael, we've got to turn you into a soldier before we let you near a drum, but after that you'll belong to one of the companies and become a man upon whom the company commander will rely."

I asked him whether he would be sorry to leave the Army. He said that it would be a wrench, but that it was time to go while he was fit and healthy enough to make another career for himself. He told me that until the end of his service he would be engaged in recruiting around the county, to make good the gaps in the ranks left by men whose time with the regiment was also coming to an end. We talked about his war with the Sikhs in India, who he said were a fierce, proud, warlike people. They had, he said, given us the hardest fights we have had since the Battle of Waterloo, but now we were the best of pals, like two lads who had had a good scrap and at the end of it realized that the other fellow wasn't so bad after all.

At length we came to Corunna Barracks, which is in the lower part of the town of Thornbury. As we passed through the entrance arch Sergeant Hancock asked the sentry whether Corporal Sheehan had come in with his party. The sentry replied that he had, an hour and more since. We then went to a room in one of the barrack blocks where we found the recruits I had seen in the village, and more besides, about twenty in all, sitting about on beds. The room was in the charge of two tough-looking soldiers called Mills and Gallagher, who were there to tell us what to do and where to go. Sergeant Hancock told them to keep an eye on me as I was the youngest present, and not allow the others to take advantage of me because of it.

My comrades were a rough lot. There were farm boys and others who could not find work, including a number of Irishmen, but there were others who were from the worst slums of the towns whose language was so foul that I could not understand what they were saying. There was a self-confessed thief who said we had nothing to fear as he did not steal from chums, and an actor called James Ainsworth who told me that no one would employ him because he was often so drunk that on stage he would recite lines from the wrong play. I was a little frightened of them all but I soon saw that everyone was just as wary of one another as I was.

Some of the men started to play cards for money on the barrack-room table. Gallagher ordered them to stop, telling them that gambling could cause bad feeling and for that reason was contrary to Queen's Regulations. One of them told him it was a private matter and nothing to do with him. At once, Gallagher hauled him out of his chair, thumped him hard in the stomach, rushed him across the room to a window Mills had thrown open, and hung him half out of it.

"Now," said Gallagher, "let's you and I understand each other before I lose my grip. Private Mills and I are the Trained Soldiers who tell you just what's what and what isn't. If we tell you to wipe your nose, you do it, right? And if we tell you not to wipe your nose, then you don't, right? What we say goes, so don't think you can answer us back any more than you can the corporals and the sergeants. Anything more you want to say, Mister Clever-Dick Barrack-Room Lawyer?"

The man shook his head and was hauled back inside. Mills, a formidable figure with a scar down one cheek and a nasty look in his eye, was towering over the card players, his fists balled.

"Anyone else like to say a few words?" he asked.

The cards were quietly put away.

"And another thing!" shouted Gallagher. "Don't get any ideas about going into town, because you won't get past the Guard Room! You're confined to barracks until we've got you looking something like soldiers, and that won't be easy! Right, now we've got that sorted out, let's get on. You each have a bed, blankets and a locker. You'll keep your bed spaces brushed and tidy and in the morning you'll be shown how to fold your blankets in a correct and proper manner."

"When do we get our uniforms?" asked the thief. Mills's face went so purple I thought he would burst a blood vessel.

"Uniforms!" he bellowed. "Uniforms! You're not fit to wear a uniform until we say so! You'll be taken to the stores where you'll be given a set of overalls, a forage cap, boots, three shirts and four pairs of socks. You'll change into them and hand in the clothes you're wearing. If you're lucky, one of the wives will give you a few coppers for them, even if all they're good for is burning!"

The man sitting on the next bed to mine was a quiet, friendly sort called Tom Wood. Puzzled, I asked him what Mills had meant about wives.

"Some of the soldiers are married," he replied, chuckling a little. "If you pay them, they'll do any extra washing you have, and some of them deal in old clothes – it all brings in a little extra each week."

In the stores one of the soldiers' wives was indeed waiting for us with the storeman. She looked me over, said she had a growing son of her own and bought my clothes for ninepence. We were then issued with a knife, fork, spoon, plate and mug each, as well as the other things Mills had mentioned.

"Lose 'em or break 'em, you pay for 'em!" snarled the storeman. After that we marched back to the barrack room where Mills and Gallagher spent some time telling us what to do and what not to do if we wanted to stay out of trouble. Two of the men they sent to the cookhouse returned with two large cooking pots called dixies. One contained rich brown stew which we mopped up with bread, and the other hot, strong cocoa. I had had no idea I was so hungry until that moment and I wolfed it down. After everything had been cleared away to the Trained Soldiers' satisfaction, I heard a bugle call.

"That's Lights Out," said Gallagher. "Blow those candles out and get to bed, the lot of you."

It seemed strange, having a bed to myself, for I had always shared with two of my brothers. I lay for a while, looking up at the stars outside the window, wondering what I had done, for surely no convicts were ever treated worse than us. Then I remembered that the family would be better off and comforted myself with the thought that things could only get better. I heard an owl hoot in the trees near what I had been told was the Officers' Mess. It reminded me of one that lived in the oak behind our cottage. Then I fell asleep.

July – September 1853

During the next few weeks I had little time to myself, we were kept so busy. Bugle calls regulated our day, beginning with the Rouse which was followed by Reveille. We then washed, dressed and folded our blankets into a neat box. I took my turn at sweeping the barrack-room floor and polishing it until it gleamed, or cleaning the washroom and the latrines. I also took my turn at going to the cookhouse with the dixies. Meals consisted of breakfast, dinner, tea and supper, all of which were eaten at the barrack-room table. The food was neither good nor bad, but it was substantial and the constant exercise gave me a mighty appetite.

Most days were taken up with drill. Sergeant Mulcahy was in charge of the recruits, who were divided into two squads of ten under two corporals. These Non-Commissioned Officers, or NCOs as they were known, had a fierce turn of phrase that would blister the ears of our vicar. They were strict but fair and when praise was due they gave it, so that we felt we were making progress.

One of the first things we were taught was how to salute the commissioned officers, but never the NCOs, and the names of those most important to us. The regiment was made up of ten companies, each with 80 men. It was commanded by Lieutenant Colonel Silas Mountjoy, who was feared but not liked, for in his black moods he would award floggings for what seemed to me to be minor crimes. We were made to watch one of these and it was not a pretty sight, for they were made with a leather cat o' nine tails that flayed the skin off a man's back. To my surprise it was always the drummers who wielded the cat. That was not a part of my duties I looked forward to, although I *was* looking forward to the day my drum training would begin.

We, the recruit squad, belonged to C Company, commanded by Captain the Honourable Martin Curtis. During our first week he spoke to us, welcoming us to the regiment in which we would soon feel proud to serve, urging us to work hard at our training so that we could earn the privilege of joining the ranks of his own or another company. He sometimes watched our progress from beside the parade ground, conferring from time to time with Sergeant Mulcahy. Our own officer, who inspected us daily, was Ensign Henry Leith – the most junior commissioned rank – who also belonged to C Company. All the officers, save for the Paymaster and the Quartermaster – both of whom were promoted after long service in the ranks – had paid large sums of money to obtain their commissions, and, in peacetime, their promotions, too.

We did not see too much of the officers, but were in constant dread of Regimental Sergeant Major Miller, who oversaw all the companies, and was the most senior soldier below commissioned rank. He could spot a fault across the width of the parade ground and whose voice, it was said, could be heard a quarter of a mile distant. To the sergeants and corporals, whom he harried without mercy, he was some sort of god, and, while paying due respect to their rank, he would even take the junior officers to task if they were late on parade or failed in some other way. We were only slightly less fearful of our own Company Sergeant Major, whose name was Hawke, who watched us like his namesake. Several times he ordered us to perform extra drill because we had been what he called "idle on parade".

The Adjutant, responsible for the administration of the regiment, was Lieutenant Carstairs. The Paymaster was Lieutenant Andrews, whose clerk I spoke to when I found I was not being paid my full 1s 2d per day. He said that there were standard deductions called off-reckonings that applied to everyone. These included laundry, barrack-room damages, replacement of equipment, and so on.

We drew our uniforms and equipment from the Quartermaster's Store at the end of our first week. I thought I would receive a drummer's white coat in addition to the scarlet one we were all given, but was told this would follow once I had joined the Drums. Our tall black hat, called a shako, was nicknamed the "Albert Pot" after the Queen's Consort, Prince Albert. It had a peak both in front and behind and a brass plate which included the regiment's badge. There were many other things for which we had to sign, including packs, water bottles, cross-straps, cleaning brushes and much else.

All our kit had to be laid out in a certain way for inspections, with the pack squared off and the shirts, socks and other garments folded to a certain size and shape in our lockers. Even our cleaning brushes had to be laid out, with the backs spotlessly clean. After duty, therefore, all my time was spent with blackball, polish and pipeclay, cleaning and polishing boots, buttons and straps. The slightest mistake, such as a spot of polish on a uniform or the inside of a buckle left uncleaned, earned a sharp rebuke and the threat of punishment if the fault was not corrected. At first, Gallagher and Mills showed us how to complete our tasks, but then, saying they were sick of playing nursemaid, they gave us no further help unless we offered them money, which they used to buy beer in the tavern outside the barrack gates.

We quickly discovered that we had to rely on each other for help, for if some of us were required for fatigue duty in the cookhouse and elsewhere, there was little time left for cleaning before Lights Out was sounded, when all candles and lamps had to be extinguished. We therefore helped each other out with our cleaning and polishing. In this way a sense of comradeship developed, for we were all aware that if a man incurred punishment through no fault of his own he could be awarded extra fatigues, or even find himself parading for inspection by the Guard Commander every two hours until Lights Out. Even those I thought to be the most evil of men when I joined appeared to be decent enough at heart, for they helped me out more than once, and I returned the favour. Tom Wood, seeing that I was having difficulty with my pipeclaying, was particularly helpful to me. He was about 22 years of age, powerfully built and good humoured. He said nothing about his past, although he knew a surprising amount about the Army and was better able to look after himself than any of us. Mills and Gallagher thought so, too, and raised the subject with him one day.

"Taken to it like a duck to water, ain'tcha, Wood?" said Mills. "I'd say you've done all this before!"

"Couldn't be you've got yourself into trouble with someone else, could it?" asked Gallagher. "Not deserted and joined us under a false name, have you?"

"You wouldn't believe me if I denied it," said Tom, grinning, "and I'd be a fool to admit it if it was true, wouldn't I?"

"Aye, you would," said Gallagher, thoughtfully. "Just keep your nose clean and you'll be all right with us."

On Sunday mornings there was always an inspection of the barrack rooms by the Company Commander, who was accompanied by the Sergeant Major. Then, Gallagher and Mills chased us round, setting us to polish the floor, clean the windows, black the fireplace and scrub the table and benches until they gleamed white. After that, there was Church Parade, which Sergeant Mulcahy told us was not compulsory, for the regiment contained some who were Methodists or Wesleyans and many more Irishmen who practised the Roman Catholic faith. At the same time he warned us that discussion of religious or political matters in the barrack room was frowned upon because it could sometimes cause trouble when people could not agree on these subjects. He said that we were the better for it, because each of us would judge his neighbour simply on the sort of man that he was, rather than the beliefs he'd been brought up with.

On Sunday afternoons we were left to ourselves, but in wet weather there was little to do for us recruits still confined to barracks. We frequented what was called the Soldier's Room where we could buy tea or cocoa and biscuits, play games such as draughts and Snakes and Ladders, or read a newspaper or a book. I liked it because it was a quiet place, free from the bawling of the sergeants and corporals. It was run by a committee of ladies from the town, in front of whom the soldiers swore or blasphemed at the peril of being sharply taken to task by their comrades. Should anyone forget himself, he was quick to beg the pardon of the ladies, who readily gave it. Nearby was a skittle alley, where it was difficult to obtain a game because it was always so crowded. We were told that not every regiment in the Army has such things, so we were very lucky. When the weather was fine we went to the sports field, where we lay on the grass and watched cricket matches between the companies.

I must confess that at times I sorely missed my home and family, and I found the restrictions on my freedom irksome, but the older soldiers all said that recruit training was one of the hardest things I would have to endure and life would seem better later. The time spent at drill seemed endless. I used to be woken in the night by painful cramps in my leg muscles, but as these muscles developed with constant use they became much stronger. At first we were drilled without arms, and then with them. The regiment had just been issued with the new Minie rifle, which replaced the old Brown Bess musket that had been in service since the Duke of Marlborough's day, and maybe longer for all I know. We learned the names of its parts, how to clean it and how to keep it serviceable in all weathers. We practised loading, without ammunition, for hour after hour until the movements became automatic, then we concentrated on improving our speed. The musketry instructors told us that the new rifle was more accurate than the Brown Bess, was effective to a far greater range and would penetrate the bodies of two men in succession, if not three.

We were marched to a small range where targets were set up against a high bank of earth, 100 yards distant, and there fired three shots from the standing position, and three more kneeling. The targets had a black bullseye, surrounded by three rings called the inner, the magpie and the outer. My standing shots scored two inners and a magpie. My kneeling shots scored two bulls and an inner, because I was better able to support the rifle. Although we were told to hold the weapon tight into the shoulder because it kicked so hard when fired, I still had a large bruise. Sergeant Mulcahy was pleased with my second target and said that in due course I should try for my Marksman's badge, which would earn me a little extra pay. Apparently we were the first in the regiment to fire the new rifle, and that made us feel superior.

We were also introduced to bayonet fighting. We were taught how to use the bayonet itself, as well as the rifle butt, how to defend ourselves against an enemy's bayonets and swords, and how to deliver a bayonet charge with a cheer that was more of a demonic yell. Many seemed to enjoy it, but I thought it was a brutal business.

"I hope it never comes to this," I said to Tom Wood after a morning spent plunging our bayonets into straw dummies.

"Don't worry, young 'un," he replied. "There's few men will dare to stand against a charge with the bayonet. Most take to their heels rather than face cold steel."

"Have you ever taken part in one?" I asked, surprised that he seemed to know so much about the subject. He smiled but did not reply.

A date was set for our passing-out parade. Our officer, Mr Leith, said that if we wished he would write to those of our families who lived locally, inviting them to watch the parade. Afterwards there would be tea, sandwiches and cake to celebrate the fact that we had become full members of the regiment. I was looking forward to seeing my family again, but, to my surprise, only about half of the men accepted his offer.

As the weeks passed, Mr Leith became more

approachable, seeming pleased with our progress. When we first joined he would storm round the barrack room at morning inspection, flinging boots into the fire buckets or equipment out of the window, telling Sergeant Mulcahy that we were a disgrace and not ready to be inspected and that he expected a great improvement when he returned in two hours' time. Sergeant Mulcahy would yell at the corporals and the corporals would yell at us, but now I believe that this was a performance for our benefit. After one such uproar I looked down from the window and saw the four of them chatting amiably together. Although he became less strict towards the end of our basic training, Mr Leith told us that before the parade could take place we must pass a Barrack Room Inspection by the Commanding Officer, who would not miss the smallest detail.

Because of the Colonel's ferocious reputation, I was dreading his inspection. On the appointed day I was up before the Rouse was sounded, cleaning, polishing and laying out my kit with extra care. Sergeant Mulcahy and Ensign Leith inspected us several times and were evidently satisfied. At nine o'clock we were standing beside our beds when we heard voices ascending the stairs. Sergeant Mulcahy called us to attention and then a regular procession entered the room. It was led by Colonel Mountjoy, who was followed by the Adjutant, then Captain Curtis, Mr Leith, Regimental Sergeant Major Miller and Company Sergeant Major Hawke. The Colonel read the card on every man's locker, examined various items of his equipment, then barked a series of questions at him. I could feel my knees beginning to shake as he approached, feeling certain that he would find some fault with me. I was aware of the Colonel reading my card and examining my kit. Then a bristling moustache and a pair of piercing blue eyes appeared in front of me, the latter boring into my skull. I kept my own eyes fixed to a point on the opposite wall, as I had been told to do.

"Your name is Pope?" he snapped.

"Yessir!" I answered nervously.

"And you have joined us as a drummer?"

"Yessir!"

"Then no doubt we shall all be hearing a great deal more from you," he said, at which the officers and sergeant majors all chuckled dutifully, for it is the drummers who also sound the bugle calls throughout the day.

"Where are you from, Pope?"

"Feldon St Mary, sir."

"Know it well. Was riding to hounds near there the other day. Pretty little village. One day we'll send you back there with a couple of medals on your chest."

Then he moved on to the next bed. I almost fainted from relief, for it seemed that I had passed. The inspection complete, the Colonel left, telling Sergeant Mulcahy that he had done well with us.

After rehearsing for two days with the band, we passed out on 5th September. Mr Leith, Sergeant Mulcahy, the corporals and the two trained soldiers all paraded with us so we all had a good feeling that we belonged together. We marched onto the parade ground in fours to the regimental quick march, "Here's to the Maiden of Bashful Fifteen". I liked this fine old tune because the beat of the drums came through so clearly. We then formed two ranks in open order and dressed by the right, so that our lines were perfectly straight yet far enough apart for the inspecting officer to pass between them. Across the square I could see the spectators, including the officers' ladies and those of our families who had come. At first I searched in vain for familiar faces in the crowd, and then, to my joy, I saw my younger brothers and sisters waving wildly. I felt proud of myself, standing there with every item of my uniform cleaned and polished to perfection.

When the Colonel and the Adjutant appeared on their horses, Mr Leith drew his sword and ordered the Present Arms. With perfect timing, our rifles were transferred from our shoulders to be held vertically in front of our bodies, while our right boots slammed behind our left ones. The Colonel returned the salute and we were ordered to Shoulder Arms. After the mounted officers had ridden slowly along the ranks, Mr Leith was told to carry on. We first marched in line past the Colonel to the regimental march, looking him straight in the eye as we had been told when we received the order Eyes Right. We then did the same to the slow march "The Duchess of Kent". Having returned to our original position, we advanced in line for fifteen paces to "The British Grenadiers" and halted. The Colonel then rode forward and said that he knew the past months had been hard work, but it had been necessary to knock the civilian out of us and turn us into soldiers. Soldiers were what we were now, he said, and we must always be proud of our calling. For his part, he was proud to have us in his regiment and knew that we would do well. Mr Leith ordered Present Arms again, then we formed fours and marched off to "O'er the Hills and Far Away".

We were then allowed to join our families in the tea tent that had been erected by the cookhouse. My father and older brothers shook me by the hand, saying I had grown and looked well, while the younger ones grinned and peered up at me. My sisters said that I would be nearly halfway to being handsome if I wasn't so ugly, at which we all laughed. I felt very proud of myself, standing there in my scarlet coat, bright buttons and polished black shako. I said I was glad to see them all, although it was a long walk both ways for the little ones, but they said that Mr Benson, the carter, had business in Thornbury and had given them a lift and would wait for them near the barracks.

Sergeant Hancock, who enlisted me, came over and joined us. He was leaving the Army the next day after 25 years' service and had come along to hear the old tunes one last time. He said that I had done well to come through my basic training, which was something that even grown men could find difficult. I was greatly pleased to hear him say this, and my father patted me on the back. Too soon, it seemed to me, it was time for our visitors to leave.

"Well, Michael, what now?" said my father as we shook hands. "When will we see you again?"

"I don't know, Dad," I replied, with a twinge of sadness. "I dare say they'll give me leave of absence for a while when I've been in long enough – that is, unless the regiment is sent elsewhere or overseas."

After taking leave of our families, we returned to the barrack room and packed our kit, ready to report to our new companies and duties. We knew we would met again but by now we had learned to know each other well and were sorry to be split up, although I was glad that Tom Wood had been posted to the same company in which I was to serve as a drummer.

October – December 1853

After the passing-out parade, I moved across to the Band block, where the drummers also had their quarters. I was made very welcome, as the drummers were below strength and their barrack duties therefore came round too often. Some of the drummers were in their twenties, but most were lads just a year or two older than me. They were a friendly lot and one of them, a 20-year-old Irishman called Paddy McGlashan, said he'd gladly show me what was required until I'd settled in.

Paddy told me that although each company had a drummer, all the drummers were known together as the Corps of Drums. We lived in the same barrack block as the Band so that we could practise together, but he emphasized that we were soldiers first and drummers second. The Band were musicians rather than trained soldiers, although if they accompanied the regiment on campaign they could be employed as stretcher-bearers. As Sergeant Hancock had told me when I joined, they seemed to have a good life, for they played at country shows, dinners and many other interesting events, whereas our duties required us to be with our companies much of the time.

My scarlet jacket was sent to the tailor's to have sleeve chevrons and shoulder wings sewn on, and I was issued with my white jacket. I was also given a white leather apron to cover my left leg when carrying my drum. The drum itself was beautiful, being painted with the regiment's crest and battle honours. I was taught how to care for it and how to keep the cords sparkling white with pipeclay. My brass bugle was also engraved with the regimental crest and had to be kept highly polished.

I was now allowed to leave barracks and I went into the town with Tom Wood and Paddy after duty one afternoon, feeling that I cut quite a dash in my uniform. I saw Polly Axworth, the daughter of a neighbour, standing outside a dressmaker's shop. She was my own age and very pretty. She was pleased to see me and I introduced her to my new friends. Soon we had a jolly gathering on the pavement. At this point her mother appeared from the shop. Apparently furious, she grabbed Polly by the elbow, trying to drag her away.

"Mother, it's Michael – Michael Pope!" said Polly, resisting fiercely. "Aren't you going to say hello?"

Mrs Axworth looked at me coldly.

"I didn't recognize you, Michael," she said. "I heard you'd gone for a soldier. Can't say I approve, but I'll wish you luck, just the same. Come Polly, we can't stand here chattering all day."

As they walked off I heard Mrs Axworth chastizing poor Polly fiercely.

"Don't ever let me catch you talking to soldiers again, my girl! They're a crowd of drunken brutes, most of them. No decent girl would risk her reputation by consorting with them…"

It was obvious that we were intended to hear these words. Tom must have seen the hurt on my face.

"You'll get used to it, chum," he said. "The only civilians with any time for us are those who've been in the Army or the Navy. The rest don't want to know us. We can only get served in the roughest pubs, they don't like us going into the shops and we are only allowed into the pit at the music hall."

"Ah, now that's true most of the time," added Paddy, who was a bit of a philosopher. "But there's also times when they really love us, Michael me boy, especially when we're off to war. There's a saying, you know, 'God and the soldier we adore, in time of trouble, not before.' You'll see, but don't let it trouble you, because we're your friends now."

I had heard of these things, but somehow had never imagined that they would apply to me, especially when they involved people I had grown up with. I had thought, mistakenly, that they would look at me in admiration, as my brothers and sisters had done after the passing-out parade, and I was deeply hurt. It was then that I first began to realize the truth of what Sergeant Hancock had told me about the regiment, with its strict routine and familiar faces, being a soldier's home and family.

Later that afternoon, we went into a small tavern called the Bishop's Head, near the cathedral, and sat round a table, looking at the newspapers that were provided. The most important item of news was that there had been a fight between Roman Catholic and Russian Orthodox monks in Bethlehem, Palestine, and one of the latter had been killed. Tsar Nicholas of Russia, who apparently prided himself on being the defender of the Orthodox faith, was trying to provoke a war with Turkey, within whose empire Palestine lay, for allowing such a thing to happen.

"Ah, that feller's out for nothin' but his own good," said Paddy. "He's got his eye on Constantinople, which is where the Sultan o' Turkey lives, an' if he gets it he'll be causin' no end of trouble for us in the Mediterranean, and maybe India, too. He needs takin' down a peg or two."

"He won't get away with it," commented Tom, glancing up from his own newspaper. "Our government says he's got to be stopped, and just for once the French agree with us. You never know, lads, we might end up fighting alongside the Turks."

I didn't think much more about the threat of war at the time, because in barracks I was kept hard at it, learning the drum calls and how to march and counter-march while playing. The great difference between life with the Drums and my early training as a soldier was that the NCOs tried to keep us out of trouble rather than make it for us. The Drum Major, Sergeant Prendergast, told me that I was making good progress but said I must master the bugle calls quickly so that I could take my turn of duty soon. He told Paddy to help me with these, for although I could read the music well enough, the calls had to be memorized and there were so many that I was inclined to mix them up.

"At one time," said Paddy, "all the signals like Advance and Retire were made on the drum, but nowadays, what with the terrible racket of gunfire and the like on the battlefield, it just wouldn't be heard, so we use the bugle instead. We have to get it right, or we'll have people goin' in all sorts of wrong directions. There are words we've fitted to most of the calls. They help us remember them because they're equal to the notes. Let's start with the routine calls in barracks – just jot them down and keep them handy."

It was much easier to remember Reveille once I'd got the words into my head. It went *Charlie, Charlie, Charlie get out of bed, Charlie, Charlie, get out of bed!* Meal Call went *Oh! Come to the cookhouse door, boys, come to the cookhouse door!* And the Post Call went *Letters from Lousy Lou, boys, letters from Lousy Lou!* Likewise, I learned the calls for the First and Last Post, Lights Out and many others. All had to be sounded at precise times during the day and night. None of the drummers had a watch of their own, so time was taken from the clock tower above the barracks gate.

In November I had to take part in a punishment parade, although, thankfully, I was not required to "wield the cat". Colonel Mountjoy, in one of his black moods, awarded 30 lashes to a man who failed to report for guard duty without good reason, 40 lashes to another for being drunk and disorderly in the town, thereby bringing the regiment into disrepute, and sentenced a third to 75 lashes plus tattooing for desertion. The tattooing instrument consisted of a brass handle which had a large number of spikes at one end. When a spring was pressed the spikes shot into the man's arm, forming the letter D, and gunpowder was rubbed into the wound, marking him for life. By the time the last lash had been given the man's back was a mass of torn flesh and blood and he had lapsed into unconsciousness, so the tattooing added little to his pain.

The sight so sickened me that I felt I had to get out of the barracks for a while. I went with Tom and Paddy to the Bishop's Head, where we drank our tankards of ale in silence.

"The Colonel's got a cruel streak in him," I said at length. "I don't think I like him."

"There's nothin' says you have to," replied Paddy. "Just respect his rank an' stay out of his way, that's best. To be sure, though, in one way you're right – the man's got the very divil of a temper on him, although to be fair to him he's never punished anyone who didn't deserve it, so maybe you're bein' a bit hard on the feller."

"There are worse," said Tom unexpectedly.

"Is that a fact, now?" said Paddy, his curiosity aroused. "And where might you have come across them?"

Tom did not answer. Instead, he tapped the newspaper he had picked up and began to read from it.

"The Russians' Black Sea Fleet has attacked and sunk an entire Turkish squadron without warning at a place called Sinope," he said. "Russia and Turkey are now at war. The Royal Navy has sent warships into the Black Sea to keep the Russians in check, and so have the French."

"Sure, we'll be in the middle of a scrap before we know it!" said Paddy.

I suppose it had been in the back of my mind that one day I might go to war, but now that it was a real possibility I became uneasy. I wondered whether I would be very afraid and, if so, would my comrades notice and, worse still, would I let them down?

However, for the moment I was more concerned about learning the tasks of Duty Drummer, for if I got anything wrong I would have the wrath of the Regimental Sergeant Major to endure, and that would be no laughing matter. Having performed the duty several times with others who showed me what to do, I did it alone for the first time on 15th November. The tour of duty lasted from Guard Mounting the previous evening until the Guard was relieved 24 hours later. I was told that the quality of a regiment is judged by its Guard Mounting. Under the Guard Commander and the NCO responsible for changing the sentries, the twelve men who took turns manning the four sentry posts around the barracks paraded in full dress on the parade ground. There they were subjected to a strict inspection by the Orderly Officer, as was the Duty Drummer and the twelve-strong fire picket, who paraded in clean overalls and polished boots and were responsible for manning the barracks' fire engine. Once the inspection was over, those on parade marched to the Guard Room to the beat of the drum and there, with much ceremony, relieved the Guard that had just completed its tour of duty. I therefore took part in both parades and sounded the bugle calls throughout the day. I was greatly relieved that I made no mistakes, although Bandmaster Mollington told me that I was a little flat during the Officers' Call.

Suddenly, Christmas was upon us. Though Guards were mounted and the cooks worked harder than ever, there were few other duties to perform, for the regiment kept the holiday in its own way. The sergeants brought us tea at Reveille. Later, the officers, including Colonel Mountjoy, served us our dinner of roast duck and plum pudding. They gave us two bottles of beer per man, then sat with us so that for a while we were all merry and bright together. On the parade ground the Band played carols, and we all joined in. The companies competed in an obstacle race and there were other games, including a blindfold wheelbarrow race in which the sergeants were made to take part, causing us much mirth as they collided and tumbled over each other. Some of the men who had served in India played a game called hockey that they had brought home with them. It was rather like football, but played with curved sticks and a hard ball like a cricket ball. I tried my hand at it and found it to be more difficult than it looked.

On Boxing Day a party was given for the children of the regiment's married soldiers and those from a nearby orphanage, to which we each gave sixpence. The children had a good tea, after which they were entertained by a Punch and Judy man, played games and were sent home with a little present and a toffee apple. This was the first Christmas I had spent away from my family and I was a little homesick. Father always made sure that the little ones got an orange apiece and a wooden toy he had carved, usually a doll or a horse. I had enjoyed myself, but I had missed all that, too, and the thought made me a little sad.

Parties of men from other regiments kept arriving at the barracks, so that in due course the regiment was said to be at full strength. There was also much happening in the Quartermaster's department, where wagons daily deposited stores. The talk was that we were to move soon. Some said to Ireland, some said to India, some said to Gibraltar or Malta, where we would be relieving regiments that would fight with the Turks against the Russians. Some said that we would go direct to Turkey, but no one really knew. Even the sergeant who ran the cookhouse was puzzled, and he was said to know everything, even before the Colonel.

I was told that in the field I was to remain as D Company's drummer. Like all the companies, it began training hard at a new fighting drill which I watched with interest. It formed a two-deep firing line, then the front rank fired a volley. The second rank passed through, halted and fired a volley while the other rank reloaded. Altogether, four volleys were fired in succession, with the ranks advancing alternately. This was then followed by an immediate assault by both ranks with the bayonet, during which I beat out the Charge on my drum. One day I heard Captain Manningham, the company commander, remark that with these tactics and our new Minie rifles we would blow away any opposition before bayonets are crossed.

On 14th February a special parade was held to mark the visit of the regiment's Honorary Colonel, Lieutenant General Sir Ledyard Crampton-Jones. The Hon Colonel did not command the regiment, but was a respected figure of great authority who could speak on our behalf to the Army's Commander-in-Chief or the Government. He had served with distinction in the regiment during the wars against Napoleon but now he was a silver-haired old gentleman, though his eyes were bright enough and he still sat on his horse with a straight back. In his honour, and so that we should always recognize them in the smoke and confusion of battle, the regiment's Colours were trooped slowly along the full length of the regiment's ranks. I had never seen such beautiful things before. There were two Colours, the Queen's Colour and the Regimental

Colour. The Queen's Colour was our Union Flag, and the Regimental Colour had the red cross of St George on a white ground. Both were made from the finest silk and were embroidered in gold thread with the regimental crest in the centre, surrounded by the names of the battles in which the regiment had taken part, which were known as battle honours. Each Colour was carried by a junior officer escorted by two experienced sergeants. Together, the Colours and their escort were known as the Colour Party.

After they had been trooped the regiment was formed into a square and Sir Ledyard addressed us in a surprisingly firm voice. He said that the Colours represented not just a rallying point in battle, but also the regiment's honour, the honour of the many good men who had died around them in the past, and our own honour, too, and that he knew they were safe in our keeping. He told us that soon we would be going overseas, and that we might be called upon to fight, although he was not at liberty to say where or against whom. He said that if there was to be a war, he had every confidence that we would give a good account of ourselves and teach the French a lesson they would never forget, which raised a few eyebrows. Then he wished us all good luck and a safe return. Colonel

Mountjoy called for three cheers for Sir Ledyard, which were given, at which the General saluted us and turned his horse away. I thought he looked a little wistful, as though he wanted to be a young officer again and come with us.

Afterwards, I asked the Bandmaster what the General had meant about the French, who I thought were of the same mind as ourselves about the Russians. The Bandmaster chuckled, saying that I should not quote him, but that Sir Ledyard had spent so much of his life fighting the French that it had become second nature to refer to all of our enemies as though they were Frenchmen, be they Indians, Afghans, Chinese or Africans.

Our last weeks in Thornbury were spent in constant turmoil, so that it was now clear that we were bound for foreign service, although we did not know where. We handed some things in to the stores and drew others out, packed some items in cases and unpacked others. The Mayor and Corporation of Thornbury, who granted the regiment the Freedom of the Town two years ago, requested that we exercise our privilege of marching through the streets to the railway station with drums beating, Colours flying and bayonets fixed. As I had not been in the Army when the Freedom was granted, I had never seen the regiment do this, although I knew that it was a tremendous honour and looked forward to it. We formed up on the parade ground with the Corps of Drums and the Band leading, then Colonel Mountjoy on his charger, then half the regiment in fours followed by the Colour Party and finally the rest of the regiment. The married men were given a few minutes to say goodbye to their families. After they had rejoined us the Colonel gave the order to march. We struck up with "Here's to the Maiden of Bashful Fifteen". Whenever the regimental march was played the men's heads came up, their shoulders went back and they swung along with pride.

As we marched under the arch above the barracks gate the Guard presented arms smartly. Then we wheeled left towards the station and were presented with an amazing sight. Both sides of the road were densely crowded with people, cheering away and waving little paper Union Flags. Perhaps I was ungrateful, but I reminded myself that these were the same people who had forced me off the pavement, refused to let their daughters talk to me, and called us drunken brutes. I felt a great sense of pride that I was a soldier and not at all like them, who hated us most of the time then loved us as soon as we were needed. I thought I saw my father and eldest brother, looking somewhat anxious, but could not be certain in that sea of faces.

We changed the tune to "The Girl I Left Behind Me", at which the crowd cheered the louder, and finally to "O'er the Hills and Far Away" as we marched into the station yard. There we halted before a dais on which the Mayor and his Councillors were sitting with their watch chains dangling across their stomachs. The Mayor made a speech wishing us well, saying that the Tsar was a tyrant who kept his people in near slavery, that he was keen to enslave the poor Turks, and that if it came to war we would certainly show him how Englishmen could fight. Behind me I heard Paddy mutter that if the fat windbag would only stop talking and come down here he would show him how an Irishman could fight, at which I nearly burst out laughing. Then there were more cheers and we boarded the train that was waiting for us.

The noise of the engine, the smell of smoke and steam and the rattle of the wheels passing over the rails were all new and exciting to me as I had never been in a moving train before. I remembered that an old man in our village had shaken his head when the railway came and said that the human body could never withstand speeds of 40 miles per hour. I am sure that we reached speeds beyond that many times on our journey without feeling any ill effects at all.

When we reached Southampton that afternoon we marched through streets of cheering people to the docks, where we boarded the troop transport ship HMT *Bombay*. This, too, was a new experience, for I had never been aboard a ship before, nor even seen the sea, which I had no idea was so vast. The ship had steam-driven engines as well as sails, though the sailors told us that the engines were only used for getting in and out of harbour or in bad weather. They also said that we were bound for Malta, but might go further, depending upon events.

I did not enjoy the first days of our voyage. The shipped rolled so badly that those who thought they had been clever in choosing the top bunk were sorry they had done so, for they were sometimes flung out on to the deck. Many of the men suffered from seasickness and the troop deck smelled horrible. One afternoon, I sought a breath of fresh air but was soon drenched with spray, for the wind was blowing a gale. The sailors, who were much amused by our plight, told me that crossing the Bay of Biscay was always rough, although we would be getting better weather soon. I was not sick, but I could not touch food for a while, and even the smell of cooking from the galley turned my stomach.

When we reached calmer waters our spirits revived. We all went on deck to see the famous Rock of Gibraltar, sticking up into the sky like a gigantic tooth, as we passed through into the Mediterranean Sea. Tom said the Rock was home to some monkeys called Barbary Apes who caused much amusement because they were so used to seeing people and would steal anything. He said he had seen one snatch a pipe out of a man's mouth, then throw it away in disgust after it tried puffing it!

In Malta, the local people came out in boats that had eyes painted on them to sell us fruit and other things. A sailor told me that we were only stopping there to take on coal and would be going on to Turkey, where the French had already gone. The harbour was surrounded by huge fortifications and was crowded

with warships of every size. Tom pointed out the
various sights around the harbour and obviously knew
his way around. By now I was becoming more certain
than ever that he had been a soldier before and
wondered why he would never talk about it.

April – August 1854

On 3rd April we disembarked at a place called Scutari, across the Bosporus Straits from Constantinople, which is the capital of Turkey, or, as some call it, the Ottoman Empire. In contrast to our green fields and woods at home, the Turkish countryside appeared brown, barren, stony and burned up by the heat.

Our regiment went into a tented camp at Scutari beside the French, with whom we got on much better than we expected. They seemed to be provided with more equipment than us, and had many more wagons and ambulances with them. We had brought out some of the men's wives, to do our washing and nurse those who were wounded, but the French had women dressed in uniform, whose business it was to supply the soldiers with wine and other items.

I could not say that I was impressed by the Turkish soldiers I saw. They wore blue uniforms and red fez hats, but had an untidy look, marched badly and were lazy. The entire camp was surrounded by Turkish traders' stalls. Tom said they would sell you anything, at a price, and it was important to haggle with them and not pay what they asked at first. When I saw some camels for the first time I went across to pat them, as one does a horse. I found, however, that they were surly beasts who hissed and spat. One caused much merriment when he stood on my boot with one of his spongy feet and tried to bite me with his dirty yellow teeth.

Shortly after we arrived, Captain Manningham, my company commander, told us that we were now officially at war with Russia, whose troops had invaded the Turkish province of Bulgaria. He said that our warships had already swept the Russian Navy off the Black Sea. The following morning the Band and Drums received orders to change into scarlet as our white coats were unsuitable for active service. Paddy said that was a good thing, too, because we drummers would have an important part to play in any battle and the white coats made us an obvious target for Russian marksmen.

Two days after we reached Scutari, Tom, Paddy and I were sent across to Constantinople with a fatigue party to pick up some of the regiment's stores that had landed in the wrong place. From across the water, the city's domes and minarets and the gardens of the Sultan's palace looked magnificent. Close to, it was a maze of dirty, smelly, crowded alleys in a state of commotion. It was all so strange that I stared about me in wonder, but then I remembered that I had been told to keep my wits about me. I had already been warned that there were beggars by the score who had to be threatened before they would leave you alone. One shopkeeper tried to drag me into his shop until Tom sent him on his way with a string of fierce oaths in a language I did not recognize.

After we had located the missing stores and taken them to the boat, Tom, Paddy and I went into a coffee shop to try the black Turkish coffee. It was served in very small cups and was too strong for my liking. Half the cup seemed to be filled with brown mud. Paddy was furious and grabbed the proprietor by the hair, knocking his fez off.

"What d'ye tink you're doin' givin' me a cup fulla dorty soil ta drink?" he shouted angrily. "I'll ram it down your gullet, an' the cup after it, if you don't give us our money back!"

"Easy, now, Paddy," said Tom, restraining him. "It's

just the way they drink coffee out here."

Paddy, muttering that they ought to know better, sat down. The proprietor, anxious not to offend his new customers further, brought us a plate of *rahat lacoum*, which we called Turkish Delight at home. It was delicious. While we sat and ate, the men sat in groups, watching us without expression while they puffed on their hubble-bubble pipes and the women stared at us with dark eyes over their veils. We felt that our money was welcome but we were not, although we had come to Turkey to help these people.

Every so often men with loud voices climbed the minarets and called the Muslims to prayer. No one appeared to pay much attention, although a few rolled out mats and knelt down on them, regardless of what was going on around them. I asked Tom why they all seemed to be facing the same way. He said that when they prayed, Muslims were required to face in the direction of Mecca, which is the holiest of their cities.

We remained at Scutari for the rest of the month, when we embarked for Varna, a town on the coast of Bulgaria. This brought us much closer to the fighting. The Russians were besieging Silistria, to the north of us, and when the wind was in the right direction we could hear their guns. But we stayed in Varna and did nothing, although we continued the regimental routine of parades, drills and exercises. I was Duty Drummer at regular intervals, and filled my time by writing home and teaching myself to swim. It was getting extremely hot and we were troubled by hordes of loathsome bloated flies and other insects. The source of these, we were certain, was the camp of the Turkish regiment whose men were too lazy to dig enough latrines for themselves and used the surrounding area as their lavatory.

By the third week of June the Russians had started to withdraw from Bulgaria. Cholera broke out in a camp near ours, causing the death of several of that regiment's men and some of our own people began to suffer from dysentery. We moved our camp to a healthier area, away from the mist that rose every night from Lake Alladyn, which some said was poisonous. The older men, who had served in India, told us that such measures were necessary, as more men died from disease on campaign than were ever killed by the enemy. But the diseases followed us, for although we moved our camp again, by the middle of July we had already lost 40 men from our own regiment of 800 soldiers. There was much grumbling among the men, who said that now the Russians were withdrawing into their own country our sole purpose in this place was to bury our comrades.

I had a dose of dysentery, during which at one point I did not care whether I lived or died. With the constant demand to empty my bowels, I could neither perform my duties nor sleep for more than half an hour at a time. My stomach would not retain food of any sort. I lost so much weight that my uniform hung upon me. Tom looked after me, insisting that I fast and drink only boiled water in which he dissolved some rice starch. After three days of this treatment, thankfully, the illness left me.

However, we continued to lose men and those who recovered were, like me, in a weakened condition. So many attended the daily sick parade that some of the companies were only at half-strength. It was said that as the Russians had now withdrawn completely from Turkish territory, it might be thought that there was no need to continue the war. However, at a regimental parade, Colonel Mountjoy told us that our governments in London, Paris and Constantinople had decided that the Tsar needed further punishment.

He said we were to break his power in the Black Sea by destroying the great fortress and naval base of Sevastopol in a province of Russia known as the Crimea, and that the generals were already drawing up plans for us to embark again aboard ship. I joined in the cheering, for by now I felt I would rather see some fighting than rot to death in the accursed place we were in, and Tom and Paddy agreed with me.

September 1854

On 5th September we embarked aboard ship once more at Varna. I cannot say that all went smoothly, for the staff officers were all in a muddle and directed us here and there until we reached the correct jetty from which boats ferried us out to our transport. I immediately felt the benefit of breathing clean air again, and so did everyone else. Our spirits rose even further when we saw the great fleet of warships and transports that had been assembled. There were ships as far as the eye could see – huge warships bristling with guns, paddle steamers, screw steamers and sailing ships of every kind.

"Now isn't that the grandest of sights?" said Paddy as we leaned together on the ship's rail. "To be sure, them Russki fellers will wish they were somewhere else when we get there! 'Tis my view we'll be eatin' our Christmas dinner snug an' warm in their very own barracks when we capture Sevastopol!"

On 13th September we were put ashore at Calamita Bay, on the coast of the Crimea near a place called Eupatoria. The name caused us much wry amusement, for our disembarkation was all higgledy-piggledy and in the wrong order, so that regiments were landed in the wrong place at the wrong time or all mixed up together. I came ashore with the rest of the company in the ship's boats, with the soldiers crammed together on the seats while the sailors rowed. We grounded some thirty yards from the shore, so that I had to wade through the shallows holding my drum above my head to prevent it being ruined by sea water. We then stood around awaiting orders for what seemed like hours. I could see that Tom was furious.

"Just look at it!" he said, pointing at the confusion taking place all round. "The only good thing you can say is that the Russian generals are even more stupid than ours! If they weren't, they'd have opposed our landing – even a small force could do us a lot of damage, the state we're in!"

Young and inexperienced as I was I could see what Tom meant. Nearby, Captain Manningham was looking through his pocket telescope, examining the country beyond the shore. It seemed to consist mainly of bare, open downland with a little farm or two here and there.

"Ha! There they are!" he said at length, almost to himself. "Patrol of Cossack lancers – scruffy looking devils!"

Sure enough, in the distance I could see the light twinkling on lance points. Below were half a dozen of the enemy in tall sheepskin caps astride shaggy horses. They made off as soon as the first of our cavalry got ashore. We then began to march inland. We were heavily laden and for those of us who had not fully recovered from the diseases contracted at Varna, the march was hard going. For some the ordeal was too much; they simply collapsed and died by the wayside. Others, gasping from exhaustion, had to be taken back to the boats for transfer to the hospital ship. When those who escorted them returned they told us that chaos still reigned on the landing beach, with stores of every kind piling up any old how without anyone knowing where anything was. It began to rain during the afternoon. We established a camp about four miles inland but there were no tents so, after we had cooked what rations we had, I rolled myself in my blanket and, using my pack for a pillow, went to sleep.

It took five days to get the whole Allied army ashore and properly assembled. On 19th September we began to march towards Sevastopol. The cavalry was on our left and the French were on our right. Our infantry regiments had been ordered to march with their Colours flying and their bands and drums playing them on. Looking out to sea, we could see the fleet keeping pace with us. In the cool of early morning it was a grand sight to see those masses of men advancing across the countryside and I was proud to be a part of it. Then, as the hours passed and the sun rose higher, the heat became unbearable. Their mouths parched from thirst, the musicians were unable to play. At length we drummers were told to desist, too, and were sent back to our own companies, for which I was grateful. By now the regiment was staggering along through the furnace temperature of the afternoon, unable to keep step. I undid my collar, and then my tunic, enabling some of the heat to escape from my body. Some men threw off their packs, for which they would surely be punished later. Others collapsed, though they caught up with us after dark.

Tom seemed strangely used to such blistering temperatures. During one of the halts he stopped me taking a long pull at my water bottle.

"A mouthful is all you need – swill it round and round your mouth until it's gone," he advised me. "Save the rest for later – you'll need it. Lick your sweat, too, because you body needs salt as well as water. And find yourself a pebble to suck – it will keep your saliva coming and stop your mouth getting dry."

I did all these things and they helped, but I couldn't help wondering how Tom knew so much. Towards the end of the day, however, both my sweat and my saliva dried up. I felt light-headed and began to suffer bouts of shivering. At dusk we halted to make camp, much to my relief. The cavalry advance guard galloped in, shouting that the Russians were waiting for us in strength on the far side of a river called the Alma, just a mile or two further on. It seemed certain that there would be a battle next day.

That evening the camp was quiet, for the men were subdued and thoughtful, wondering what lay in store for them. I didn't want to be killed, but the idea of losing a leg or an arm frightened me more. I didn't want to seem afraid, although I had no idea how I was going to stop myself. Most of all, I didn't want to let anyone down, for I would have to live with that for the rest of my life.

"Worried?" said Tom, reading my mind as we rolled

out our blankets on the hard ground.

"I'm not sure what to expect," I replied, unwilling to betray my nervousness.

"Nor do any of us. It won't be pleasant, but pay no attention to what is happening to everyone else. Just do the job you've been trained to do and you'll be fine."

I wasn't convinced and sat silently poking the ground with a stick.

"There's a wise saying the Muslims have," said Tom at length. "If something happens to you, they say, then it's because 'it is written', meaning your fate is already written in a big book in Heaven. For us soldiers, it means we'll either come through a fight or we won't. Either way, there's nothing we can do about it. If it's any help, most men do come through a battle."

"Thanks, Tom," I said, feeling a little better, then I rolled myself in my blanket. I began to accept the fact that my fate no longer rested in my hands.

I was ordered not to sound Reveille next morning, but had no idea why. As the dawn broke we had a hasty breakfast of coffee and bread, then formed ranks. For a while nothing happened. I asked Captain Manningham why we did not advance and he said we were waiting for the horse-drawn ammunition train to come up so that the men's pouches could be filled. This took until ten o'clock. We then moved off with the rest of our brigade - made up of four regiments. We advanced slowly across scrubland, with frequent stops to ensure that our own companies remained level with each other, and that our regiment was level with those on either side of us. I do not know the exact time, but I think that it must have been after one o'clock that we breasted a rise and saw the Russian army arrayed along the heights on the opposite side of the valley of the River Alma. I could see large formations of grey-clad infantry whose bayonets gave off a continuous sparkle in the sunlight, and also some entrenchments that contained guns. After we had advanced some way down the slope towards the river, our company columns deployed into a two-deep fighting line with the Colour Party in the centre of the regiment. My heart began to thump and I was breathing hard, knowing that very soon the fighting would begin. We were preparing to move off again when the Brigade Major galloped up to Colonel Mountjoy and told him that we must halt awhile as the French were not ready to begin their attack. At that moment, there were puffs of smoke from the Russian earthworks. Seconds later, some fountains of earth were thrown up ahead of us. We were ordered to lie down, as the enemy would have corrected his aim next time he fired.

It seemed like an age, lying there waiting for the order to continue our advance. All the while, from the heights beyond the river, the Russian artillery fired upon us and from the front we heard the crackle of musket fire as our skirmishers pushed theirs back. Cannonballs passed over our heads with a sound not unlike tearing cloth and struck the ground in front of us, throwing up earth. Those who had been in action before warned the rest of us that even when they look harmless and are just rolling, we must not try to stop them, lest we lose an arm or a leg. The Russians were also using shells that burst overhead in a thunderclap and sent splinters raining down. At first I was not afraid, for the men talked and laughed among themselves, even when they were showered with soil. Then we began to suffer our first losses. A man was flung backwards out of the line like a rag doll, his body smashed to red pulp by a ball. Others were struck by the flying splinters, one of them giving a scream I shall never forget as the hot shards of flying metal cut into him. Then a shell, its fuse fizzing, dropped between the feet of Jim Ainsworth, the actor who had joined the regiment at the same time I had. It exploded almost at once, blowing off his legs. Poor Jim was killed instantly. It was the sight of his exposed thigh and hip bones, white and shining, that made my stomach rebel. Not wishing to show my fear, I looked round for somewhere to be sick, only to find Company Sergeant Major Caldicott, who seemed not to worry about the enemy's fire, standing behind me.

"Face your front, Drummer!" he said, sharply. "If a ball's got your number on it, it will find you wherever you are! So sit tight and make yourself comfortable while you can. We'll be off again soon."

What would I have given then to be back in my own village of Feldon St Mary, where such horrible sights have never been dreamed of.

I couldn't see Tom as he was further along the line, and began to wonder how Paddy was getting on in his own company. Ten minutes later the Brigade Major appeared again and we resumed our advance, for which I was grateful, though I knew we were moving into even greater danger. Our brigade was to cross the river to the right of a village. This was now burning fiercely so we were forced even further to the right and got mixed up with a French regiment. For a while their blue uniforms were so mingled with our scarlet that there was no way of knowing where one regiment ended and the other began. On the far bank there was a terrible muddle as we sorted ourselves out from the French. We were now within range of the enemy's muskets as well as his artillery. Men were starting to drop, but Colonel Mountjoy would not allow us to advance further until the companies were properly formed and the ranks straight. He rode from company to company reminding us of the tactics we had practised at Thornbury.

"Remember, lads, I want four sharp volleys off you! After the fourth volley the buglers will sound the Charge and in you go with the bayonet!"

As we began to climb the slope I looked to the left. The Russians seemed to have beaten off our first attack there, but our regiments had rallied and were coming on again. All the drummers were beating the Advance as we climbed. I was terrified, but drumming served to take my mind off the numbers of our men who were falling as we climbed upwards, creating gaps in the ranks.

"Close in! Close in to the right!" the Sergeant Major kept shouting, and the gaps were filled as the men moved into them.

Being near the centre of our line I was close to the Colour Party. I saw the Regimental Colour fall but it was raised again immediately. Suddenly, the enemy guns ceased firing. Looking ahead, I could see the reason. A huge column of Russian infantry was moving slowly down the slope towards us with the bayonets of their front rank levelled. There was a terrible menace about those figures in their long, grey greatcoats and tall, spiked helmets. Suddenly a wild-eyed staff officer galloped up to us, pointing at the column.

"Don't fire!" he was shouting. "For God's sake don't fire! That column is French! Bugler, sound the Retire!"

I replied that I only took my orders from Captain Manningham, who immediately told the officer to clear off and stop making a nuisance of himself. The man galloped away, still shouting his head off.

"It's all been too much for the poor fellow!" Captain Manningham said. "His nerves seem to have given way!"

Only 100 yards separated us from the Russians when the Colonel gave the order to halt.

And then came a second order. "Front rank – fire!"

A tremendous volley crashed out along the length of

the regiment's line. The fearful effect of the Minie rifle was clear at once, for the two front ranks of the enemy column were sent reeling.

"Rear rank, advance – fire!"

The next two enemy lines were tumbled into ruin.

"Rear rank, advance – fire!"

The result was the same. Although the smoke was thickening, I could see that the Russians had been brought to a standstill and some of them were trying to protect themselves by pressing back into the body of their column.

"Rear rank, advance – fire!"

I immediately sounded the Charge. Led by the officers waving their swords, our regiment surged forward with a tremendous cheer. I followed as fast as my drum would allow, drawing my short sword. Only a few brave, or rash, Russians made a stand and they were soon dealt with. The rest turned and fled. In the exhilaration of the moment I was almost sorry that I had not had to fight. We pursued the Russians up to the crest of the heights and beyond until I was ordered to sound the Recall.

"Well done, my boys, well done!" said the Colonel, and we gave him three cheers. Everywhere the Russians were in flight. On the crest I came across some strange articles, including a top hat, a lady's fan, and a picnic basket, the contents of which I shared with those nearby. Speaking in French, a captured Russian officer told Captain Manningham that the best of Sevastopol society had come out to see the fun, then departed in all haste when matters did not turn out quite as they expected. We laughed heartily when the Captain translated for us.

Then came the sad business of attending to our own losses. I looked round for Tom but, to my horror, I could not see him. I obtained Captain Manningham's permission to look for him. The slopes we had ascended were covered with the scarlet figures of our comrades. Some were beyond assistance, others were being carried or assisted down to the river, at the mouth of which lay the hospital ships. It was with great sorrow that I came across the body of Ensign Leith, who had carried the Regimental Colour.

It was clear that if the enemy had been armed with rifles, like ourselves, instead of smooth-bore muskets, the tally of our dead and wounded would have been much greater. The Russians lay thick upon the ground where we had destroyed their column. Some of their wounded stared at us impassively, others with real hatred in their eyes. I saw one of our men give a drink to a wounded Russian from his water bottle. As soon as he turned his back, the Russian reached for his musket and shot him dead. The treacherous Russian fellow was finished off immediately, and we took the further precaution of smashing the stocks of every Russian musket in sight. They were not all barbarians, however. I gave some assistance to a wounded officer. One of his legs had been smashed and he had been shot through the body twice. In excellent English he told me he knew that he was dying and asked me to make him a little more comfortable, which I did. In return he insisted that I take his watch, which was a fine repeater that pinged the number of the hour just past when a button was pressed, saying that it would only be stripped from him if I did not. This was true, for some of our men were already taking rings and other items from the dead, commenting that it was part of a soldier's due. Inside, the watch was engraved. I could not read what the words were, for they were in Russian characters, which have the look of our own letters held in front of a mirror.

I continued my search for Tom, and saw that the silver drums of the enemy littered the slopes around me. Some of their drummers had been killed but the rest threw them away when they ran. I knew that it was almost as much a disgrace for a regiment to lose its drums as it was to lose its Colours. The sight of a dead Russian drummer of about my own age made me realize how lucky I had been.

At length I discovered Tom, lying halfway down the slope. A musket ball had struck the brass plate of his shako, penetrated the leather behind, then cut a furrow across the top of his head. To my relief, he was alive but unconscious, and covered with blood. There was more blood soaked into the left side of his tunic, where a second ball had grazed him. I tried to move him as he was lying uncomfortably with his head downhill, but was unable to until I received help from a sergeant and corporal of the Queen's Fusiliers who were making their way down to the river.

"Good Lord, it's Joe Parker!" exclaimed the Corporal, looking at Tom in astonishment.

"His name's Tom Wood, Corporal," I said.

"No, son, it's Parker. I should know, as I served alongside him for four years in Africa and India," said the Corporal.

The Sergeant was bending over Tom. I saw a flicker of recognition cross his face, then his expression changed.

"Aye, there's a resemblance, but he's not Joe

Parker," he said to the Corporal. "Take another look – what would Parker be doing here, anyway?"

The Corporal did as he was bid, then the two of them exchanged meaningful glances.

"You're right, I was mistaken," said the Corporal. "Least said, soonest mended, right?"

"Nothing said is better still," replied the Sergeant. "Come on, let's sort him out, whoever he is."

Together, we bandaged Tom's wounds and then they went on their way. I was puzzled by the way they had recognized him, then quickly decided that they had been mistaken. More than ever, I was convinced that Tom had been a soldier before, and now it seemed that the Queen's Fusiliers formed part of his mysterious past. Shortly after, the Band arrived with their stretchers. I saw Tom lifted safely on to one of them and then returned to the top of the hill.

The elation of victory passed quickly. For most of us, this was our first real experience of war and the horrible sights and sounds of it began to affect us.

That evening, the company was sitting quietly round a camp fire, talking little. Paddy came across from his own company to see whether I was all right and I told him about Tom. "I'll betcha a penny to a pig that in England they'll be ringin' the church bells an' talkin' o' glory," he said, more or less to himself. "Now wouldn't it be a blessing if them what starts wars could see for themselves what glory looks like close to." No one answered, but I think we all agreed with him.

Because of his wounds, which were not serious enough to require evacuation, Tom remained with the regiment's baggage train for ten days after the battle. When he returned I told him how the two fusiliers had mistaken him for someone called Joe Parker, but changed their minds. He looked at me with his eyes narrowed for a minute, but said nothing. I had a feeling that whatever the secret he was keeping to himself, it was dangerous.

During that time we marched around Sevastopol and began to lay siege to the city. Under the direction of the Royal Engineers we dug out positions from which our big guns could batter the Russian defences. These positions were called parallels and were to be dug so close to the defences that an infantry assault could be launched from them. They were protected by gabions, which were large circular wicker frames filled with earth, and by sandbags. Each new parallel we dug was closer to the enemy than the last and they were connected by zigzag trenches leading forward.

I usually spent a day or a night in the trenches, before joining a daily carrying party which went down to Balaklava harbour and brought up rations, ammunition and other supplies to our lines, a journey of seven miles each way. Loaded down as I was, I found that the return journey was hard work as it was mostly uphill, and I required frequent halts to recover my breath. The French had much the better of the bargain here, for Balaklava harbour lay at the end of a steep gorge, whereas they had two convenient harbours situated much closer to their camps, and plenty of wagons to carry their supplies.

One day while we were working in the trenches we received a visit from Lord Cardigan, who commanded the Light Brigade in the Cavalry Division. His Lordship was wearing the uniform of the 11th Hussars, whom he had commanded until recently, remarkable for its distinctive cherry-coloured trousers. He was accompanied by a TG and Colonel Mountjoy, who introduced them both to Captain Manningham. TG stood for Travelling Gents and was our name for rich civilians who had come out to watch the War. They wandered round the camp and the trenches, poking into everything and generally making a nuisance of themselves. This TG's name was Pomeroy Clarke. He was a foppish fellow who affected a sort of lisp. He minced about, trying not to get his polished shoes and clean trousers dirty in the mud of the trench, then peered out of a gun position we were constructing.

"I say – Wussians!" he said, pointing towards the enemy working on their fortifications.

"I should get down from there if I were you," warned Colonel Mountjoy. "That is, unless you really want a bullet through your hat."

"Heh, heh!" sniggered the TG. "Something to show the chaps at home, what? Couple of holes through the old topper, eh?"

He then turned his attention to me.

"Ah, a bugler feller! Tell me, do you blow that thing vewy vewy loud?"

"Yes, sir," I replied.

"So loud the Wussians can hear you?"

"I believe so, sir."

"Well, that's dashed unfortunate, I think, because they'll know just what's going on. Much better if you blew it quietly, what?"

The man was obviously a complete fool. I dared not

answer him back as I should have wished to, so I pretended to be as stupid as he was.

"Why no, sir. You see, all the calls I blow are in English, and the Russians don't speak a word of it!"

For a moment there was silence, then Lord Cardigan burst out laughing.

"Haw haw haw!" he chortled. "Damme, Pom, if the young feller hasn't got you there! Give him a guinea – no, make it two, for it's worth it! Blows his bugle in English, what? Haw haw haw!"

Puzzled, the TG handed me two guineas and left with His Lordship. There was even a twinkle in the Colonel's steely eyes as he patted me on the shoulder before following them. He had mellowed since the regiment came on campaign.

"Pope, isn't it? Well done. Keep an eye on him, Manningham – given the chance he may go a long way."

Captain Manningham was also pleased by the episode, but warned me against doing that sort of thing too often. When we got back to camp the story had become common knowledge and I was grinned at by all and sundry for having got the better of a TG. I now had two guineas in my pocket though nothing upon which to spend it. But so far, the weather had been kind and on the evenings we were in camp we were able to relax from our hard work and listen to the regimental band for an hour or so.

October 1854

At the beginning of October we began constructing platforms and protected positions for our siege guns. I was greatly excited when these monsters were hauled into position and looked forward to the moment when they would open fire, for it seemed to me that they would soon reduce the Russian fortifications to ruins. On 18th October they opened a tremendous bombardment, along with the French guns and the guns of the fleet, which was lying off the harbour entrance. When the Russians replied, the noise was such that it was impossible to speak without shouting. The regiment was not required in the trenches until the afternoon, so Tom and I found a vantage point on high ground to watch this tremendous spectacle. There were constant gun flashes from our siege batteries, and from the Russian fortifications, which were being knocked to pieces. Dense clouds of powder smoke drifted everywhere. Likewise, the Russian fire was causing damage to our batteries and trenches and I could see a constant stream of stretcher-bearers carrying the wounded to the dressing stations to the rear. At half-past ten, there were two huge explosions in the French lines that shook the earth and sent a towering column of flame, smoke and earth high into the air.

"What was that?" I asked Tom.

"That was bad news for us," he said, grimly. "The Russians have hit one of the French powder magazines. There must have been tons of gunpowder and ammunition stored in there, which means that the French won't be able to continue with their share of the bombardment."

Sure enough, the French fire dwindled away, although our own guns kept up their attack. By afternoon, the fort opposite us, called the Redan, had been reduced to a ruin. The regiment was marched into the trenches, where we were formed into a column of assault and given scaling ladders by the Royal Engineers. Fear began to churn in my belly as it had before the Battle of the Alma, but at the last moment we were informed that the French were not ready, so the assault was cancelled and at dusk the guns fell silent.

At dawn I was awoken by Tom, who had been out with a patrol during the night. He told me to look through one of the loopholes in our sandbag parapet. To my astonishment, all the damage we had inflicted yesterday morning had been repaired, and all the guns we wrecked had been replaced. Tom said that the whole population of Sevastopol must have turned out to do the work, for he distinctly heard the voices of many women and children inside the Russian defences. As the company came out of the trenches later that morning we passed one of our siege batteries that was about to open fire again.

"What's the point in firing off precious ammunition if you people don't attack?" shouted an angry gunner at us. "All our hard work's been for nothing!"

"You forget it's us who have to hump your precious ammunition all the way from Balaklava!" someone yelled back.

I could hear the officers talking about the situation among themselves.

"I fear that after the explosion of their powder magazines yesterday the French will be unable to launch an assault for some time," said Captain Manningham. "We're not strong enough to attack on our own, so that means staying put where we are until they have made good their losses. The problem is, the longer we allow the Russians to keep strengthening their defences, the more difficult it will be for us to storm them. Somehow, I don't think we'll see the inside of Sevastopol until next year."

I was bitterly disappointed to hear him say this. Paddy had said we would eat our Christmas dinner in the Russians' barracks, but if Captain Manningham was right that didn't seem likely.

At dawn on 25th October we had just returned from a night in the trenches and were hoping for some sleep when the sound of cannon fire came from the direction of Balaklava. Just as I was rolling myself in my blanket, a staff officer galloped through our lines towards our divisional commander. Then there was a mighty scurrying to and fro as the brigade and regimental commanders were summoned. Shortly after, Captain Manningham shouted for me to blow the Fall In followed by the Double. Like everyone else, I wondered what was going on. There was much grumbling in the ranks, for we were very tired.

We began to march hard towards the sound of the guns. Most of the time we marched at the double and I had been told to leave my drum behind or I would not have been able to keep up. At length we reached the edge of Sapoune Ridge where we stood, breathless and sweat-soaked, while the generals decided where we were to fight. To our left was Lord Raglan, our army commander, and his staff, one of whom was scribbling on a notebook. He tore off a page and handed it to an aide who disappeared over the edge of the plateau at a break-neck gallop.

Far below I could see the Balaklava Plain, which looked flat, although it was divided into the North and South Valleys by a long, low ridge called Causeway Heights. From where we stood, we could see right down the North Valley, and the South Valley was to our right. There was drifting smoke here and there, but I could make out the French coming up on our left, and I could see masses of Russian cavalry drawn up at the far end of the North Valley, behind a battery of guns. There were more Russian guns on both sides of the valley, and infantry, too. Our own cavalry were just below us, with the Heavy Brigade some distance to the right and rear of the Light Brigade. The Light Brigade consisted of light cavalry regiments, including hussars, light dragoons and lancers, while the Heavy Brigade contained dragoons and dragoon guard regiments – made up of big men on big horses.

Suddenly I saw the aide who had been sent down the near-vertical slope in front of us with the order from the staff officer. He was galloping hard for the group of officers that revealed the position of Lord Lucan, the commander of our Cavalry Division. After a few moment's conversation Lord Lucan sent for his two brigade commanders, Lord Cardigan and General Scarlett. There was some conferring, then they returned to their troops. I could see Lord Cardigan make some changes in the position of his regiments, then, when they had dressed their ranks to his satisfaction, he rode out in front of them.

The notes of the Advance floated up from the bugles far below, then both brigades began to advance straight up the North Valley. "I'll be damned!" shouted Captain Manningham to Lieutenant Bourne. "What the deuce are they playing at? They'll be cut to pieces before they've covered half a mile!" Lord Raglan and his staff were also shouting at each other and pointing. Even I, young and inexperienced as I was, could see that our regiments were about to ride into a fearful crossfire from the guns on either side of the valley.

A figure – I think it was the aide who had carried the order – tried to overtake Lord Cardigan, but in that instant a shell burst near his horse, which galloped back through the ranks of the Light Brigade while the rider slid from his saddle, dead. Then all hell broke loose as all the enemy guns seemed to open fire at once. The Light Brigade all but vanished into an inferno of dust and explosions, leaving behind a growing trail of dead, dying and wounded men and horses.

"Look!" shouted Tom, who was standing beside me. "There's a little dog going in with them!"

Sure enough, there was a small dog running for all he was worth alongside one of the Light Brigade regiments. Lord Lucan had now halted the Heavy Brigade, which was retiring slowly out of range. Colonel Mountjoy shouted that we were to occupy Causeway Heights as quickly as possible. We set off down the steep track, scarcely looking where we were going, for all our eyes were fixed on the terrible spectacle taking place below us in the North Valley. The Light Brigade was being shot to pieces, but now, lance points gleaming and sabres flashing, its regiments had broken into a wild, headlong charge for the battery of Russian guns at the end of the valley. It seemed that there was no power on earth that could stop them. Together, the guns belched smoke and flame one last time, blowing yet more gaps in the ranks, and all we could see in the smoke was the slashing of sabres. The smoke began to clear.

"They've taken the guns!" was the incredulous shout. "Look, look! They're attacking the Russian cavalry!"

We could not see the details, but it was clear that the brigade's survivors had ridden through the battery like a tidal wave and were setting about the massed ranks of the Russian horsemen behind the guns.

"Oh, you stupid, brave fools!" said Captain Manningham. "Haven't you done enough already?" I could see that there were tears in his eyes, caused perhaps by anger or pity or both. By the time we reached the foot of the hill the Light Brigade had begun to return in small groups along the valley, subjected to almost as much terrible fire as they had endured during their charge.

Our regiment now formed up in line. I took my place beside Captain Manningham as we began to advance towards Causeway Heights. There was a sudden shout of "There go the French!" A French cavalry regiment was launching a charge along the northern slopes of the valley. They scattered the Russian infantry, cutting them down, and causing the enemy artillerymen to hitch up their guns and head for safety. From Causeway Heights, however, the enemy continued to fire, while squadrons of their Cossacks wheeled out across the valley to cut off the Light Brigade's survivors. However, the latter were still full of fight and the Cossacks, who were in fear of them, just jabbed uselessly at them with their lances and were swept aside, unless they came across a wounded man on foot, whom they were happy to spear.

We had reached Causeway Heights when the Light Brigade's survivors returned to our end of the valley. Some had come through unscathed but others, men and horses alike, bore terrible wounds. I shall always remember the crack of the farriers' pistols as they put down horse after horse that was beyond help. One day, I hope, there will be no need to involve these noble animals in war. We broke ranks to help those men we could, and would have risked a dozen floggings to do so, but we were not reprimanded. I felt a fierce pride in those who had ridden in that terrible charge, sent to near certain death yet caring little for the terrible risks, and was honoured to shake the hand of some of them. They spoke of giving the Russians "a damn good hiding" and said they would do so again if they dared to show their faces. When the fit men rallied to reform their regiments, however, we were greatly saddened to see how small these had become.

I came across an 8th Hussar, tying a bandage around a rough-haired terrier, the same dog we had seen running alongside his regiment during the charge. "This is Jemmy," said the Hussar, who himself had a bloodied bandage tied around his head. "Came with us all the way, and came back too. Collected a couple of shell splinters, but we've got those out. Proper soldier now, ain'tcha, Jemmy?"

The dog, whose coat was matted with blood, wagged his tail with pleasure. I was still tickling his ears when Captain Manningham ordered me to sound Fall In. We advanced along Causeway Heights, but by then the Russians had had enough and were withdrawing. I came across the bodies of many Russian cavalrymen and later learned that during the morning the Heavy Brigade, though outnumbered many times, had charged the enemy on that spot and trounced them until they fled to the far end of the North Valley. Most of the enemy seemed to have died from sabre cuts to the head. I saw more Russian bodies in the South Valley, and beyond them, near a village called Kadikoi, close to the start of the Balaklava gorge, the thin red line of one of our infantry regiments. I was told that they were the 93rd Highlanders, and that the Russian cavalry had tried to ride over them into Balaklava but changed their minds when they received a couple of smart volleys.

When I asked Captain Manningham what the battle had been about, he said that the Russians had a field army in the Crimea as well as their troops in Sevastopol, and that this had been trying to capture Balaklava with a surprise attack.

"We should have been in a pretty pickle if they had," he said. "It's the only British harbour and we should have lost all our supplies."

We remained on Causeway Heights overnight but when the enemy retreated next day we returned to our camp. All the talk was of the Light Brigade and the magnificent charge it had made. Tom said that he had been talking to one of the Hussar sergeants, who told him that the Brigade had begun the charge over 600 strong, but now less than 200 men remained mounted, so great had been the slaughter of horses during and after the charge. It was also being said that the charge should never have been made in the first place, and that someone had blundered. This frightened me, for I believed that our generals would never waste the lives of good men, or good horses, and now they had made serious mistakes costing both.

November 1854

After the battle at Balaklava I resumed my familiar routine of duty in the trenches in front of Sevastopol, as well as the endless carrying parties. When I returned to camp from the trenches on the morning of 5th November I was soaking wet, for it had rained all the previous night and was still drizzling. There was a mist so thick in places that one could not see more than three yards ahead. As we all settled down to breakfast, the church bells in Sevastopol were clanging. To our ears the noise was discordant, for the Russians did not peal their bells as we did at home, but rang them all together. At first, we thought that it was one of their religious festivals, but the sound of heavy firing from Mount Inkerman, at the head of Sevastopol harbour, told us that something serious was happening. I was told to sound Fall In and then off we went through the fog towards the sound of the fighting. We were simply told to stop the Russians, whatever the cost. As at Balaklava, I left my drum behind because of the need for haste.

Mount Inkerman consisted of a series of rocky, winding ravines surrounding a mountainous plateau, but as we marched everything was concealed by a dense blanket of mist and I could see nothing of it. There were sounds of movement all around, but whether they were made by friend or foe we had no idea. We had advanced only a little way along the plateau when we blundered into the Russians, or they into us, I do not know which. They were wearing the same long, grey greatcoats I had seen before, but had discarded their spiked helmets in favour of flat-topped caps shaped like muffins. We discovered from their insignia that they were the same regiments that we had fought against at the Alma, so they were no longer strangers to battle, and they wanted their revenge upon us for making them run away and lose their honour.

There was no time to be frightened. The company let fly with our volley first, tumbling their front ranks, then went straight in with the bayonet and a tremendous yell. It was savage fighting, with no mercy being asked or given by either side. After a few very long minutes, the Russians melted away into the mist. But then another group appeared, and another, looming blank-faced out of the grey mist, so that the same fight took place over and over again. It was like a horrible dream that would not go away. At first I used my drummer's sword. It was too short to strike or thrust with, having been designed for ceremonial purposes, but I could parry thrusts and occupy one of the enemy until one of my comrades dispatched him. Then, during a lull, I put away my useless sword and armed myself with a discarded rifle and bayonet. The old hands say that long fights with the bayonet are rare, as one side or the other usually gives way before it comes to that, but on Mount Inkerman that day we crossed bayonets with the enemy more often than not. I believe that what is called the "red mist" was upon many of our men. They fought with teeth bared and blind fury in their bloodshot eyes, not caring whether they were killed or wounded. They say that at such moments the brain works at terrific speed, and one's reactions are like lightning. I cannot remember everything that happened, nor do I wish to. I do remember that at one point Captain Manningham was surrounded by four or five of the enemy and knocked to the ground. He would have been bayoneted if Tom had not raced forward and stood over him, swinging his rifle like a club to keep the Russians at bay until a party of us rushed to their rescue.

I think it was during the next fight that I took on a Russian twice my size. I rushed at him with my bayonet, but he was quick with his parry. My training had taught me that he would follow through by bringing the butt of his musket round hard to strike me on the side of the head. Instinctively I stepped back, but tripped over a body and fell. I saw the look of triumph in the man's eyes as he closed in for the kill. I thought that was the end for me, but then someone shot him. He collapsed on top of me, leaving me completely winded but otherwise unharmed. Tom dragged me free and I was able to get my breath back.

As the morning wore on, the mist began to thin and finally to clear, revealing the enormous odds we faced as more Russian columns advanced along the plateau towards us. In our company, Lieutenant Bourne and many other good men had been killed, while others, sorely wounded, were making their way to the rear. By now the company had become split into groups that had lost touch with one another. I had lost sight of Captain Manningham so I stuck with Tom, who seemed to be taking control. "Over here, boys – give us a hand!" he shouted to stragglers from other regiments, who were keen to fight under anyone who would lead them. More and more of them joined us, so we still presented a firm front. Tom told me to sound the Advance as he thought that this would fool the Russians into believing that we were bringing fresh regiments into the fighting line.

During the brief lulls in the fighting, we watched in admiration as our artillery shot great gaps in the enemy's packed ranks. They were heavily outnumbered by the guns that the enemy massed on Shell Hill, which was situated at the far end of the plateau, but our gunners endured shot and shell without flinching as they worked around their weapons. They fell steadily, and gun after gun was shattered or bowled over by the Russian fire, but still they concentrated on breaking up the columns that were attacking us, with no thought for themselves. At length, we were forced back by sheer weight of numbers. For a moment, our guns were lost to the Russians, though the gunners fought like fiends to defend them. By now, however, more of our regiments had joined us and together we counter-attacked, driving the enemy back once more. It was shortly after this that I saw two of our big 18-pounder guns being hauled up on to the plateau with tremendous effort by large teams of men. As soon as they opened fire the Russians on Shell Hill began to get a taste of their own medicine. After a few minutes during which their guns were sent flying and an ammunition wagon blew up, they brought up their horse team and began to head for the rear, having decided that they had met their match. Deprived of the support of their guns, the Russians seemed to lose heart. We were too exhausted to press them hard, but suddenly I heard unfamiliar bugle calls being sounded to our right. For a moment my heart sank, as I thought that the enemy was about to attack us with fresh troops. Then rank after rank of soldiers dressed in baggy red pantaloons, blue waistcoats and red fezzes came into view. I recognized them as one of the French zouave regiments, raised in North Africa, which I had seen in their camp. We cheered them and the way they went at the Russians was enough to put the fear of God into Old Nick himself, although their charge cost them a considerable number of men.

Nevertheless, the enemy was withdrawing slowly and sullenly. By early afternoon Shell Hill was in our hands again. We could see the Russians streaming back into Sevastopol or across the Tchernaya river. Gradually our scattered and sorely tried regiments sorted themselves out. For a while we just sat on the ground, so drained in body and mind that it was difficult to think, let alone talk. The battlefield was like a butcher's yard. Bodies lay everywhere, sprawled in the open, piled in the ravines or scattered among the rocks and scrubs. When we had been pushed back earlier in the day, the enemy had killed those of our own wounded we had been forced to leave behind. As for their own wounded, many lay there with hatred in their eyes and would gladly have done us harm if we had not become used to their tricks and smashed their weapons.

I remember just sitting, staring at my boots for a long time. They were cracked, split and worn down from hard use. Our company cobbler had died in Varna and none of the other cobblers in the regiment had any leather to work with. Then I spotted a Russian officer of about my own build lying dead nearby. I walked across, measured his foot against mine, decided that his boots would fit me, and took them. The Russians make excellent boots of soft leather, far better than I could ever afford at home. Then, from his pockets I took a gold cigar-case and a purse containing gold coins. Such acts had disgusted me at the Alma, but I was even more disgusted by the way the enemy had killed our wounded and thought that the proceeds could be put to good use for my family when I got home.

As I sat on the battlefield, I thought about how the mist had played a strange part in the fighting. If we had known how many of the enemy soldiers there were, perhaps we should not have attacked them with such gusto – and if they had seen how few we were, they would certainly have pressed their own attacks much harder. The Russians were as brave as us, but there was something amiss with them, for whereas we would fight under the nearest officer or NCO, once their officers were down and there was no one to tell them what to do, they faded away into the fog.

Eventually, feeling heartily sick of war, I went and sat by Tom. He was wiping his bayonet clean with a handful of grass. His face and uniform were splattered with blood, but it was not his own. When he glanced round at me I could see that he was completely exhausted.

"Are you all right, young Michael?" he said in a weary, expressionless voice.

I nodded, but said nothing.

"I know what you're thinking, and you're right," he continued. "It was just plain butchery from start to finish, the worst I've ever seen."

He was about to go on, but at that moment Paddy strolled over from his own company. As always, he was able to make the best of things.

"'Tis glad I am to see the pair of ye are still walkin' about on yer legs!" he said. "Now, wasn't that a hullabaloo and a half? Faith, I've not cracked so many heads since I was at my cousin Deirdre's wedding in Galway!"

Paddy was doing his best to be cheerful but, try as I might, I could not respond because of the shock I was feeling in the aftermath of this terrible battle. Tom said that hot food and a good night's sleep would help to put it behind us. We remained where we were until we were relieved at dusk, then marched back to camp. On the way we passed the Queen's Fusiliers, formed up beside the track. Their colonel stared hard at us, then walked forward towards Captain Manningham.

"Halt your men, if you please, Captain!" he snapped.

Captain Manningham did as he was bid. The Colonel's face was the most evil I have ever seen. It reminded me of a gargoyle we had on our ancient church in the village, but it was fleshier. He walked directly to Tom, who remained staring straight ahead.

"Parker, isn't it?" he said. "Thought you could escape me, did you? Well, you've earned yourself a thousand lashes for your trouble!"

"My name is Wood, sir," said Tom, flatly.

"Your name is Parker, sir!" snarled the Colonel. He turned to Captain Manningham. "This man is guilty of desertion and assaulting a senior officer, Captain. I'll take him off your hands and give him what he deserves!"

"I believe that you are mistaken, Colonel McVeigh," replied the Captain replied, evenly. "His name is Wood and deserters do not fight as he fought today."

"Dammit, sir, don't you bandy words with me!" roared McVeigh, his face purple with rage. "You will hand him over!"

"I shall not, sir. I suggest you discuss the matter with Colonel Mountjoy, with whom I believe you are acquainted."

"Have a care, Captain," said McVeigh, his voice now a vicious whisper. "You will not cross me twice, I promise you!"

Captain Manningham ignored the threat. With an abrupt "By your leave, sir," he saluted the Colonel and gave the order for us to march on. I glanced at Tom. His expression was one of relief. However, his past had finally caught up with him and I was terrified of what might happen if he fell into McVeigh's hands, for a thousand lashes would almost certainly kill him.

When we got back to camp I told Paddy what had happened and we agreed that Tom needed all the help we could give him. We found him sitting behind our tent lines, looking sad and thoughtful as he chewed on a stalk of grass.

"The word is ye've troubles aplenty, Tom," said Paddy. "If ye'll talk to yer friends it will go no further, an' mebbe they'll be able to do somethin' for ye."

Tom said nothing for a minute, then took the stalk out of his mouth.

"I'll tell you a story about a friend of mine called Joe Parker," he said. "Joe belonged to the Queen's Fusiliers. He served with them in Africa and India. It was a happy regiment then, and Joe had reached the rank of corporal. Well, when they came home, their old colonel retired and in his place they got Colonel Tobias McVeigh. Now, you might think that Colonel Mountjoy is a holy terror, but if he's strict he's also fair. McVeigh, on the other hand, was a cruel, drunken bully, a madman who punished unjustly and enjoyed it. When his own officers tried to reason with him he made their lives hell, so the best of them left. He was so hated and feared that the regiment had more desertions in his first six months than it had had in the previous six years."

Tom paused while he thought what to say next.

"One day, when Joe was Corporal of the Guard, he was sent to the Colonel's house with a message," he continued. "He found McVeigh in the stable yard, drunk as a lord and thrashing some poor stable lad for not cleaning his boots properly. Joe said enough was enough, at which the Colonel told him to mind his own business. When Joe picked the lad up and told him to make himself scarce, McVeigh struck him across the face with his whip. Joe clouted him good and hard, as he was entitled to, but he came back for more and they had a scrap, at the end of which McVeigh was knocked cold."

"What happened to Joe?" I asked, knowing I was referring to Tom himself.

"McVeigh had him court-martialled for striking his superior officer. There were no real witnesses. The Colonel's servants said they found Joe standing over McVeigh, which was true enough. The stable lad had been given money and warned what to expect if he told the truth, so he said he had run off when Joe arrived and didn't see what happened next. Anyway, the court smelled a rat, so all Joe got was the loss of his stripes and a year's detention. To cut a long story short, the two men escorting him to the detention barracks were on Joe's side and all three of them deserted."

"Ah, now if I'd been yer friend Joe, wouldn't I have headed for Australia or Canada or America, as far away as I could get?" asked Paddy.

"That's what the two men in the escort did," Tom replied. "Joe, on the other hand, was of the mind that if you wanted to hide a piece of straw you'd put it in a haystack, and therefore the last place you'd look for a deserter would be in the Army." He paused again, then laughed bitterly. "Joe was wrong," he said.

I didn't know what to say. Tom had been a good friend to me more than once and I was frightened at what might happen to him, just because he had tried to do the decent thing. It seemed so unfair, and I couldn't think of a single thing I could do to help. It was Paddy who eventually broke the silence.

"Isn't that the divil's own luck, now?" he said thoughtfully. "To be sure, though, if anyone comes here lookin' for yer friend Joe Parker, they'll not find him. There's plenty here will speak up for ye, an' from the sound of it there's more than a few of the Fusiliers would do the same. And what's more, if the matter got desperate, there's some would chance their arm to see ye safe out of it."

All we could do for the moment was wait and see what happened.

A couple of days after the battle on Mount Inkerman I was Duty Drummer at the regimental headquarters tent. In the middle of the morning, Colonel McVeigh arrived, bringing with him three of the Queen's Fusiliers, including the sergeant I had met at the Battle of the Alma. I had no doubt what McVeigh's business was about and, sure enough, a runner was sent to fetch Tom, who was marched into the tent by the Regimental Sergeant Major. Although I had been sent a little distance away, it was impossible not to hear the two colonels bellowing at each other. I began to warm to Colonel Mountjoy as I heard him defending Tom.

"Don't you march in here making demands, McVeigh!" I heard him shout. "I doubt if there's a man in your regiment you haven't flogged half to death, so if you think I'm handing over this man without proof of what you say you're much mistaken!"

"Ha! I've got all the proof you need waiting outside!" replied McVeigh, a note of triumph in his voice.

They emerged from the tent, followed by Tom and

the Regimental Sergeant Major.

"Is this man Corporal Parker or is he not?" shouted McVeigh at the three Fusiliers, pointing at Tom.

"He is not, sir," said the sergeant.

"No, sir," said the second man.

"I've never seen him before, sir," said the third.

McVeigh's face turned so black with fury that I thought he would explode. He cursed the three Fusiliers horribly and stalked off. I thought I saw Tom exchange a brief look with the sergeant.

"Wood, you're improperly dressed!" said Colonel Mountjoy, unexpectedly. "I'm told that you did remarkably well on Mount Inkerman the other day, so whether you are Corporal Parker or not, you are now Corporal Wood. Go and sew your stripes on!"

"Yes, sir – and thank you!" said Tom, grinning with relief and pleasure.

"A word of advice," continued the Colonel. "My friend Colonel McVeigh is the senior regimental commander in the brigade. If anything happens to the brigade commander he will take over. It will then be more difficult for me to defend you. I think you understand."

I think we all understood and hoped that this would never happen.

A day or so later the weather become much colder. Although Captain Manningham had predicted it, I do not think that our elderly generals expected to fight a winter campaign, for all we had to protect us against the weather were our tents and the uniforms in which we came ashore. These were now so worn that we had to patch them with whatever was to hand. Our shakos were battered and shapeless so we wore our round forage caps most of the time. There were insufficient carts to bring up supplies from Balaklava to the camp and we seemed to be wet, tired, cold and hungry most of the time.

We were spending four nights out of seven in the trenches and some of the men's health began to suffer. Our old friends cholera and dysentery returned, taking off several victims each day. By way of contrast, the French had huts to live in and they were well supplied because they had brought plenty of wagons with them. They also had a good hospital and many ambulances, whereas we had neither. We began to feel that we were their poor relations and wondered how such a state of affairs could have been allowed to happen.

On 14th November a wind of hurricane force arose shortly after dawn and continued until the afternoon, accompanied by torrential rain. Every tent in the army was flattened. The air was filled with flying hats, coats, blankets, mackintosh ground sheets, papers and personal possessions of every kind. I saw tables and chairs blown along as though they had no weight. Terrified cavalry horses broke their lines and scattered far and wide. So difficult was it to stand upright that we were forced to huddle together behind a low wall, watching our belongings vanish across the landscape. The only building in the area was a small farmhouse used by Lord Raglan as his headquarters, and even this lost part of its roof. Although we were able to put up our tents again, the camps had become a desert of trampled, ankle-deep mud. In Balaklava harbour ships were driven aground or sunk with their cargoes aboard. Trying to draw supplies from the commissaries' stores there was difficult enough before, but after the great gale it became impossible as no one knew where anything was or who was responsible for it.

Every day it seemed to rain, sleet or snow. It became impossible to dry my clothes properly. Many times I thought about my family, snug and dry in our cottage, gathered round the log fire, and wished I was with them. It was painful to think on it, but here I was in the Crimea and there was nothing to be done about it.

December 1854

By the beginning of December things had gone from bad to worse. For several days there was no issue of tea, coffee or sugar. Fuel for our fires was in such short supply that what we had was given to the company cooks so that we could have at least one hot meal a day, usually when we got back from the trenches. There was driftwood to be had in Balaklava harbour, but we could not bring out much of it as we were so heavily laden with ammunition and rations. Whenever we went down to Balaklava we passed the surviving horses of the Light Brigade, standing ankle deep in mud and shivering because of the biting wind. The artillery had already taken the best of them to make good its own losses.

One day, as I was going down to Balaklava with a carrying party, Jemmy, the terrier who had taken part in the Charge, came up to me, wagging his tail. As I bent down to pat him, his master came over.

"Your horses are in a sorry state," I said.

"They're starving to death," he replied, sadly. " The

trouble is that the generals insist that the cavalry must be kept here in case the Russians attack again, although the poor animals are useless for any kind of work."

"But there's plenty of fodder in Balaklava, just a few miles away," I said.

"Well, it might just as well be on the moon, for we need tons of it every day and there's no means of getting it out to us."

"Why can't the horses be led into Balaklava at night?" I asked.

"Ah, now you're talking common sense," he replied bitterly. "That's not a thing some of those running this War know much about. I've seen some of our lads in tears because they can't do more for their horses, aye, and some of the officers too. Still, at least I can see young Jemmy here gets a share of what I get each day."

We returned from the trenches of Balaklava in our wet clothes and slept on the wet ground, huddled together for warmth under damp blankets. There was no comfort to be had in our tents, which leaked. When it snowed, we used it to build walls around our tents to break the force of the wind. For weeks I had not taken off my clothes, which were now little better than rags. Although we received some reinforcements, our numbers dwindled daily because of sickness. Those of us who had been here since the campaign began had got used to our hardships, but many of our reinforcements, unused to these conditions, fell sick soon after they arrived. By mid December we were not only suffering from cholera and dysentery, but also from scurvy, foot-rot and frost-bite. Foot-rot was caused by standing in trenches that were no better than muddy ditches and, like many others, I suffered from it. As my feet could not be dried for long periods, the skin became soft and white then peeled into bleeding cracks. I was in pain for most of the time and found it difficult to sleep but considered myself lucky as some men lost fingers or toes from frostbite and one or two sentries were even found frozen to death.

In the second week of December, a man in a rifleman's patrol jacket visited us. He was Mr William Howard Russell, the correspondent of *The Times*, of whom I had heard. The generals did not like him because of what he wrote about them, but I heard our own officers say that he was right to report the dreadful conditions in which we had to live, so that those at home would know. Mr Russell told us that the beggars in London fare better than we do. We laughed and said we should give a great deal to sleep in a dry doorway.

By the third week of December the strength of the regiment fell to less than 200 men fit for duty. Because of this the company was now in the trenches six nights out of seven. We were terribly tired, but no man would report sick unless he had to because it meant that someone else would have to do his duty. The carrying parties drained the strength from us. With my feet hurting every step of the way, I staggered along scarcely knowing whether I would get to my destination – Balaklava or back to camp. The country carts the army purchased in Bulgaria were never built for such hard use and began falling apart. When one broke down, its contents were quickly plundered and it was broken up for firewood, so we were forced to carry even more. The track to Balaklava was littered with dead horses and mules. Most of the Light Brigade's horses were now lying dead in the mud. The rest, starving, gnawed on each other's manes and tails. All that can be said is that the Russians cannot have been much better off than we were, because there was very little firing between us.

During a search for fuel I found myself close to the

French lines. One of their drummers, about my own age, beckoned me over. Neither of us could speak the other's language, but with much laughing and gesticulating we somehow managed to understand each other. He said his name was Marcel Ducros and his father was a farmer. I told him who I was and where I came from. He showed me his drum, which was as fine as mine, and we compared the calls we had to beat. I was invited to sit down with his comrades around their fire and was given a portion of what they call *soupe*, which was really a stew in which meat and vegetables were cooked together in one pot. It was eaten with a portion of fresh bread, and, famished as I was, it tasted like food for the gods. Some of them spoke a little English. They seemed like good fellows and were sorry for us. When their young officer came along I respectfully stood up but he told me to sit down. Like all French officers, he addressed his soldiers as *mes enfants*, which meant "my children". This seemed strange to me, as he was younger than most of them. He gave me a bottle of wine to take back, saying that it would warm me up. I shared it with the seven remaining men in our tent – by this time, the rest of the original sixteen had either been killed or taken off to hospital suffering from wounds or disease.

Our own rations consisted of salt beef or pork, ships' biscuit and green coffee beans. Those who had lost their teeth due to scurvy had trouble with the biscuit, which they had to soak in order to break them with their gums. We were also issued with cakes of hard chocolate, about the size of a flat cheese. We were uncertain whether we should eat this or make drinks from it, and thereby made a marvellous discovery. We had made a small fire in the tent, surrounded by stones. Tom accidentally dropped a piece of chocolate into the fire and it began to burn fiercely. We quickly placed our green coffee beans in a sock, pounded them to powder between two stones, placed the sock into our can of water and, using the rest of the chocolate as fuel, we made ourselves a good mug of coffee.

These hard times strengthened the feeling of comradeship throughout the regiment. Colonel Mountjoy, whom we used to fear, showed himself to be a man of kindness and consideration after all. He visited us often when we were in the trenches, talked to us and knew most of our names. He insisted that the sentries had a strong pull at his brandy flask to keep out the cold. One day, he brought a Sardinian general round, the Italian Kingdom of Sardinia having joined the War on our side.

"These are the same men who stormed the Heights of Alma," I heard the Colonel say. "Look at them now! They have been used most shamefully, sir. I am not without friends in high places, and I shall make it my business to see that heads roll because of this."

"It would be better still if those responsible were sent here to live as we have to," said Captain Manningham bitterly after the Colonel had gone. "Then they could experience for themselves the results of their stupidity!"

"Surely, sir, it is not the fault of Lord Raglan?" I said. "He does not seem the sort of gentleman who would allow his soldiers to be treated like this."

"No, he is not," the Captain replied. "Nor are any of the generals here. They do the best they can, but it is the system that defeats them. You see, the Army is not the responsibility of just one government department. There are separate departments for guns and ammunition, for supply, for medical services, for purchasing and heaven knows what else. Those who run these departments make little empires out of them, recruiting clerks by the score and creating hundreds of forms to justify the work they are supposed to be doing. The departments believe they exist for their own benefit and not for ours. They squabble constantly among themselves, and their petty quarrels seem more important to them than anything we might need."

He paused for a moment, then continued, "They are all represented here. As you well know, when we go down to Balaklava, our requisitions for stores have to be signed by the right man. They have to be given to the right man, if he can be found. When he is, he will issue a docket to his clerk. The clerk will check his ledgers to see if the stores exist. If they do, they have to be found somewhere in the chaos along the quays. And when they are found, they may be buried under tons of other stores, which have to be moved. Then, once we have signed for our stores, there is the problem of getting them back to camp or the siege lines without carts and with too few men to carry them. The Russians could do no more to hinder us if they tried. However, there are signs that changes are on their way, so let us be thankful for that."

At least Mr Russell's dispatches seemed to be having some effect. The public may not have cared for us much when we were at home, but their letters in the copies of *The Times* that we received told us that they were shocked at the way we were being treated. Despite this, two disgraceful events became common knowledge and caused much anger throughout the entire army.

Shortly before Christmas, a ship reached Balaklava loaded with warm and waterproof clothing, woollen socks, mufflers and knitted jackets, all provided by kind people at home at their own expense. The wretched commissaries could not agree who should take responsibility for unloading and distributing these items, so they remained aboard the ship. Likewise, a consignment of brand-new greatcoats was unloaded into a barge so that it could be landed the faster, but was not covered with a tarpaulin. The commissary concerned was not available at the time, nor was he told of their arrival for some days, during which it snowed steadily. The greatcoats were reduced to a sodden, useless heap.

During this time I tried to remember what it was like to be warm and kept moving as much as possible, although my feet hurt more than ever. Whenever I was off duty I rolled myself in my damp blanket and exhaustion soon brought sleep, but after an hour or so

I would be woken by cold and cramps and feel so stiff from hunching myself together that I could hardly move.

At the company's morning parade on 23rd December Captain Manningham said that he had two sad pieces of news for us. The first was that Major Pemberton, the regiment's second-in-command, had died of cholera the previous day. The second was that he, as the senior captain, was to take his place, and that meant leaving us. I was sorry to hear about Major Pemberton, although I had rarely seen him, but sorrier still that Captain Manningham was going, for he was liked and respected by us all. He added that our remaining officer, Ensign Adair, was to be promoted lieutenant and assume command of the company. Mr Adair was about the same age as Captain Manningham, but he could not afford to purchase his promotion in peacetime, so I was pleased for him. At the same parade a new officer, Ensign Farrell, joined us, looking a little out of place in his clean uniform. He had not long left the Royal Military College at Sandhurst and was about eighteen or nineteen years of age. He seemed pleasant enough, was keen to learn and was a little in awe of those of us who had been here throughout the campaign.

My dysentery returned at Christmas and refused to respond to treatment. I knew I was also suffering from something else as for several days I suffered periods of severe sweating or shaking with cold so badly that my teeth chattered. My eyes began to play tricks on me. Everything was either in sharp focus or began to swim in front of me. My head throbbed constantly. When I tried to speak the words wouldn't come out properly and I saw Tom looking anxiously at me.

One morning, at about the time of the New Year, we were relieved in the trenches. The company prepared to march back to camp, but I could not move and simply sat in the mud at the bottom of the trench.

January – February 1855

I have only slight impressions of what happened to me in the early days of 1855. I have memories of being jolted in a cart and feeling the slow rolling motion of a ship. I was aware of being stripped of my clothes, sponged down and fed with a spoon. From time to time, it seemed that people gathered round me and I heard voices whispering, some of them female.

When I came to I was no longer cold or wet and was lying snug in a warm, dry bed. I was in a long, darkened room lit by oil lamps turned down low. Along each side of the room were beds in which many more men were sleeping. Above each bed was a board on which was written the man's name, rank and regiment. At the end of the room was a door through which a light was shining. I had a sudden memory of my mother telling me that the Norse people had an ancient legend about a place called Valhalla, to which warriors went after they had died. For an instant I thought I was dead and sat bolt upright, but then a familiar voice spoke my name.

"Ah, Michael, me boy, ye're awake at last!"

It was Paddy, my old friend from the Drums, smiling at me from the next bed. I wondered if he, too, was dead.

"Where are we? What are we doing here?" I cried.

"We thought ye was a goner for a while," said Paddy. "Welcome back."

The light emerged from the door at the end of the room and came towards us. It was a lamp, being carried by a lady. Her dark hair was parted in the middle and covered by a scarf, and her dark dress had a white collar. She put the lamp on the locker at the foot of my bed and came to examine me.

"You are in hospital at Scutari," she said in a firm but gentle voice. "You have been seriously ill with a fever, but it has broken at last. You must now rest and recover your strength, and not start gossiping with your friends."

"Where is my uniform, miss?" I asked, looking down in surprise at the nightshirt in which I was dressed.

"It was in rags and no longer fit to wear, so it was burned. You'll be given another one when you leave us."

"But I had a fine pair of Russian boots, a gold watch and other things," I said in alarm. "What has happened to them?"

"Don't worry," she replied. "The ward sister has them all safely put away for you. Now you must try and sleep."

She settled me down, adjusted the sheets and pillows, and left as quietly as she had come.

"Who was that?" I asked, for she was nothing like the soldiers' wives who were sometimes required to perform nursing tasks. They were kindly in their way, but had little medical knowledge beyond the changing of wound dressings, whereas this lady was educated and had a quiet air of authority.

"That was Miss Florence Nightingale," said Paddy. "If it were not for her and her ladies, there'd be many more of us here kicking up the daisies by now."

After that I drifted into a long, deep sleep from which I did not awake until the following afternoon. I was terribly weak and was not allowed to move from my bed for several more days. Then I was allowed up for a few hours each day. I was surrounded by men from every regiment in the army. Paddy said that when he arrived a week or two before me the hospital was still trying to cope with the wounded from Inkerman and that the huge numbers of sick arriving came close to swamping it.

"They say that at first the surgeons and the orderlies wouldn't let Miss Nightingale and her ladies near the wards," he told me. "In the end, there was so much work they were forced to. Ah, ye should have seen the way they started chasin' the orderlies around! Aye, and tellin' the surgeons what was what! Now, it's the doctors do the doctorin' an' the nurses who run the wards, and isn't that the way it should be?"

Paddy went on to say that the number of those dying had dropped steadily. Some of the wounded who had recovered but were unfit for further service because they had lost an arm or a leg, had been sent home. Others, including those recovered from wounds or sickness, had been returned to their regiments.

By the beginning of February I was allowed up for the day. Like the rest of those who were recovering, I helped the nurses by handing out food at mealtimes and doing other odd jobs. They had a quick, bustling step and were constantly busy, but they always had a cheery word of encouragement for us. The soldiers thought the world of them and were very respectful. At this time, I also wrote to my family, explaining why they had not heard from me for a while, and telling them not to worry.

Miss Nightingale had set up a quiet reading room for us. Most of the newspapers were out of date, although they gave us a fair idea of what was going on. As many of the men could not read, I read to them, and most of the news was good. Thanks to the public outrage at what we had endured, the government had fallen. It had been replaced by one which had promised to reform the way the Army was run and break the system that nearly destroyed us. Better still, thousands of pack animals had been purchased from far and wide, including oxen, mules, camels and buffaloes. They had brought piles of warm, waterproof clothing up to the camps from Balaklava and had taken the place of the wretched carrying parties that had half-killed us. Huts had replaced our tattered, leaky old tents and gangs of specially recruited navvies had created a decent track out of the rutted lane leading down to the port. A railway had been started that would one day stretch all the way from Balaklava to the plateau. Many of the men chuckled when they heard all this, saying they wished they had been in Balaklava when whoever it was sorted out the commissaries and their clerks, because it must have been a sight for sore eyes.

Eventually, Paddy went back to the regiment, and in a fine new uniform, too. There were, however, still plenty of men from the 110th remaining in the hospital. Sergeant Mulcahy, who commanded my recruit squad, walked into the reading room one day. He had arrived here shortly after me and was also on the road to recovery from dysentery, although he looked much thinner than when I saw him last. I told him how poor Jim Ainsworth had been killed at the Alma and asked him if he knew how the rest of our squad were getting on. He said that Gallagher, one of the trained soldiers who had been responsible for our barrack room, was now buried on Mount Inkerman, but he had lost track of the others, although he was sure there were some of us still about. I wondered how Tom was getting on and was relieved when a recently arrived soldier from our own company told me that he had come through the worst of the winter and was all right the last time he had seen him.

In due course, I was passed as fit by the doctors and issued with a new uniform. Like many before and after me, I left the hospital at Scutari feeling that I owed Miss Nightingale and her ladies a debt of gratitude I could never repay.

March – June 1855

I rejoined the regiment on 5th March. It was a different world from the one I had left. The weather was dry and getting warmer. Everyone had new uniforms, the huts were comfortable and we had plenty to eat. We now had more warm clothing than we needed as *The Times* had started a Crimean Fund and chartered several steamers which had recently reached Balaklava. They were loaded with warm clothing of every kind and much else besides. I was astonished by the generosity and kindness of the British people. Whole villages had packed trunks containing warm items and had included toffee, soap, pots of honey, brushes, combs, jars of ginger, pencils, potted meats and peppermint lozenges. With them came little notes, sometimes simply addressed "To a soldier," wishing us well, and those of us who could write were encouraged to reply. I wrote to a Miss Mary Cottrell, who lived in Feldon St John, only three miles from my own village. I hoped she would write again, for we all looked forward to getting letters, even those among us who could not read. I told her that if she was ever in Feldon St Mary she should call on my family. She would be sure to get a warm welcome because I had also written to them telling them of her kindness.

On my way up to our lines I saw the new railway, which had reached the village of Kadikoi. The gradient of the railway track was so steep that the trucks were hauled by horses or teams of seventy sailors in harness. When I reached the regiment's camp I received a warm welcome from Tom and Paddy, who told me that thanks to reinforcements and men returning from the hospital, we were only on duty in the trenches three nights out of seven.

The fighting had begun again. By day the big guns fired steadily at the Russian fortifications. They did considerable damage, but each night the Russians worked like ants to repair and improve them until they seemed stronger than ever. We were positioned opposite the Redan fort. We believed that we could have taken it easily if our assault in the autumn had not been cancelled, but since then it had been enlarged and strengthened. The Royal Engineers, who were the experts in these matters, told us that all approaches to the Redan were now covered by fire from adjoining enemy fortifications, and that whoever carried out the assault in due course would have a hard time of it. Sometimes, usually at night, the Russians made a sortie to attack one or other of our siege batteries and put the guns out of action. On one occasion I spotted them forming up in No Man's Land and was able to sound the Alarm in good time. The result was that we shot down many of them and those few that actually broke into a nearby battery were either killed, driven out at the point of a bayonet, or made prisoner.

The Russian snipers had also become a menace during the day, picking off the engineer officers with our working parties in No Man's Land. Mr Adair had a scarecrow made. It was dressed in an old red coat and a shako and it was raised above our breastworks from time to time. Sure enough, the snipers fell for the ruse and shot at it. The powder smoke from their muskets gave their positions away and next time they showed themselves, our own marksmen dealt with them.

One day, in early April, a van drove into our regiment's lines. The civilian driver jumped down and asked me whether he had reached the camp of the 110th. I replied that he had, and, wondering what his business was, asked him what he was selling.

"I'm not here to sell you anything," he said, laughing. "My name is Roger Fenton and I am here to make photographs."

"What are they?" I asked, puzzled. By now Tom and a few others had come out of our hut, curious about what was going on.

"If you put a glass plate treated with certain chemicals into a box called a camera," Mr Fenton explained, "a lens in the box will record on the plate whatever the camera is looking at. The plate is then treated with more chemicals and the image is there for all to see."

He showed us several examples, including scenes from the trenches, our generals, and our Allies, then made a photograph of us in a group, telling us to remain perfectly still while he did so, as it took some time for the chemicals to work. He said he made a photograph of some Turks last week. They would have killed him had not their officer prevented it, for when they saw the photograph they swore he had stolen their souls and was a child of Satan! We laughed heartily, but I was still amazed when he developed our picture and showed it to us.

In May I received letters from my family and also an interesting note from Miss Mary Cottrell. She said that she was sixteen years of age and was in service at Templeton Park, the home of Sir Gervase and Lady Templeton, which is situated about halfway between our two villages. Her father also worked for Sir Gervase and knew my father, to whom he took wheels for repair from time to time. She asked when I should be coming home, but I could give her no answer. Many of us were asking the same question, for we felt that it was about time we brought this siege to an end. All of my family were well and my father had been persuaded to charge more for the excellent work he does, so things were a little better for them.

Mr Adair was proving to be a good company commander. From time to time he called us together and told us how the War was going elsewhere. Early in June he told us that an Allied expedition had captured a town called Kerch.

"As you know, the Crimea is almost an island," he explained. "Kerch is a town lying at its eastern end, covering a strait which separates the Crimea from the

Caucasus. This strait provides a passage from the Black Sea into the Sea of Azov. Our own gunboats, and those of the French, have entered the Sea of Azov and are having great success in cutting the supply lines of the Russian field army and the garrison of Sevastopol, depriving them both of food and ammunition."

At this we cheered, for without supplies the Russians in Sevastopol could not hold out for ever, and the end of this miserable siege began to seem a little closer.

During the second week of June our heavy guns increased their rate of fire and we learned that at last we were to launch an assault. I began to be troubled by the same doubts and fears that I had had before the Battle of the Alma, although I understood that if we succeeded it would probably mean an end to the War.

The plan was that we should attack the Redan on 17th June while the French attacked another strong fort called the Malakoff to the right of us. The 110th Regiment was to lead the assault against one face of the Redan with ladder parties of strong volunteers who would erect the ladders against the walls of the fort when they reached the ditch surrounding it. The ladder parties would be followed by stormers, who would fight their way into the interior of the fortifications. I was to sound the Advance as soon as the ladder parties reached the ditch.

It seemed that the Russians were waiting for us. As soon as the ladder parties began to run forward across open ground, guns opened fire upon them from every angle, cutting them down. At Mr Adair's order I blew the Advance and the stormers swarmed out of the trenches. They picked up the ladders and continued to advance against the fort, but men were falling all round me. I am certain I saw the Russian infantry, several ranks deep, firing into us from the ramparts. Then a large shell exploded nearby. I was thrown through the air and must have landed on my head, for I lost consciousness.

When I came round the firing had almost stopped. I had a swelling the size of an egg on my head and my left arm hurt where it had been grazed by a musket ball. I tied a handkerchief around it until the bleeding stopped. I seemed to be alone, save for the dead, and guessed that our men had retired to their own trenches. I decided to follow them but was dizzy and confused as to which way to go as there was still plenty of drifting smoke about and the shellfire had wiped out all the familiar landmarks. I stumbled into the area over which the French had made their attack, and saw that they had fared as badly as we had, for their dead and wounded lay all around. I came across a smashed drum and, sprawled nearby, my friend Marcel Ducros, the drummer who had invited me to share his supper during the winter. Although I did not speak his language, it was obvious that he was in great pain and asking for my help. As he had been shot through both legs, I hoisted him across my shoulders, conscious that the firing here was still quite heavy.

When I reached the trenches and handed over my burden, the French officer seemed astonished to see me. I asked him for a paper to prove I had not run away, which he willingly gave me, asking me for my rank, name and regiment. As it happened, I did not need it, for men, wounded and otherwise, were still coming in from No Man's Land at nightfall.

The regiment had suffered severely. Colonel Mountjoy was dead. He was among those who reached the fort's ditch and was shot down while encouraging the ladder parties. I had feared him once, but had come to like him and was sorry he had gone, for he was the father of the regiment and it would seem strange to be without him. There were, to my sorrow, many other familiar faces I would not see again. Sergeant Major Caldicott having been killed in the attack, Sergeant Mulcahy joined our company as sergeant major. We had also lost two of our three sergeants and Tom was appointed acting-sergeant to replace one of them. On the day after the battle a truce was arranged so that the battlefield could be cleared of dead and wounded.

Our confidence was severely shaken by our failure, but there was more bad news to come. On 25th June Lord Raglan died. It was said that after all the battles we have fought and all we have gone through, the failure of the attack on the Redan finally broke his heart. The British Army in the Crimea was now commanded by General Sir James Simpson.

July 1855 – April 1856

In July, our big guns again began hammering the enemy's defences for all they were worth. They were having the desired effect, for the Russians began deserting to us in numbers we had not seen before. Some of them said they could not stand the bombardment, from which they were losing between 300 and 400 men each day. Others told us that food was becoming scarce in the city and could not last much longer.

One morning Mr Adair told me to report to regimental headquarters at noon sharp, where I was to appear before Major Manningham, who was now commanding the regiment. I asked him whether I had done something wrong, but he simply smiled and would say no more.

When I arrived the Regimental Sergeant Major huffed and puffed over the state of my uniform, as I expected he would, then marched me in to Major Manningham's office. A French general was there. After I had saluted he began to read in French from a paper, which the Major translated as follows:

"On 17th June 1855, Drummer Michael Pope of the British 110th Regiment of Foot, while returning wounded from the attack on the Redan, came across Drummer Marcel Ducros of the French 55th Regiment, who had been shot through both legs and was unable to move. Disregarding his own injuries and the fact that he was still under fire, Drummer Pope carried the wounded Drummer Ducros to the safety of the French lines. In recognition of which Drummer Michael Pope is awarded the Medaille Militaire.

By order of General Pelissier, commanding the French Army in the Crimea."

The General then saluted me, pinned the medal on my chest and, to my horror, kissed me on both cheeks. Confused, I stammered that I was only returning a kindness and was sure Drummer Ducros would have done the same for me. Major Manningham and the General laughed, saying that did not alter the facts of the case and, having shaken my hand, sent me on my way. Back at the company, my hand was also shaken many times, although I also received a lot of good-natured joshing from my comrades.

A week or so later I received letters from my family and Miss Mary Cottrell. Her father had taken her with him when he delivered a wheel to my father, and she met my sisters, to whom she took a great liking. My sisters' letters said that they liked her and that she is pretty. I was suddenly sick for home, the quiet English countryside in summer, and the friendly faces I knew. I comforted myself with the thought that the end of this business could not be far off, enabling us to quit this shell-torn wilderness.

On 17th August there was a battle on Traktyr Ridge, above the Tchernaya river. The Russian field army attacked the French and Sardinians there but retreated after five hours' fighting. We were not called upon, and for this I was glad, as the reinforcements we received from England were of poor quality. When I say they were boys, most were older than I am, but, as Sergeant Major Mulcahy said, I had become an old hand in terms of experience. The new arrivals were neither properly disciplined nor trained, having been sent out too early by their depots.

By the beginning of September it had become obvious that we were going to mount another attack on the Redan and the Malakoff. Our brigade commander, Brigadier Miles Deighton, visited our trenches one morning to take a closer look at the Russian lines through his telescope. By the worst possible stroke of luck, a Russian shell burst immediately in front of him, and he was killed instantly. We were all saddened by this because he was well liked, but suddenly I realized what else his death would mean and I sought out Tom.

"You know this means that Colonel McVeigh will take over the brigade," I said. "You could be in trouble before you know it."

"You're right – he's a man who'll hold a grudge for ever," he replied. "I'd sooner take my chance fighting the Russians than the thousand lashes he's got in store for me. I'd better make myself scarce for a while."

Sure enough, the next day the Provost Marshal came looking for Tom with two of his sergeants. However, most of the old hands knew of Tom's problems and they sent them on one wild goose chase after another. They were told he was in the trenches, but when they got there they were told he had just gone down to Balaklava, and in Balaklava they were told he had gone back to camp, and when they got there they were told that he had been wounded by a sniper and evacuated to Scutari the previous week. Finally, the Provost's party gave up and returned to headquarters.

Two days later, on 8th September, we were formed up ready to assault the Redan when Tom suddenly reappeared and volunteered for one of the ladder parties. At the appointed hour Mr Adair gave me the signal to sound the Advance and we surged out of our trenches towards the Redan. The result was much the same as in our previous attack. Scores of us went down under the Russian fire, but we eventually reached the fort's ditch. Beyond this our recently arrived reinforcements, who were little better than recruits, would not go, although the ladders were being placed against the wall. The Russians quickly overturned the ladders or shot those trying to mount them, leaving us no alternative but to fall back. Tom was cursing the recruits horribly, and the latter were hanging their heads in shame. We were all mixed up together with the Queen's Fusiliers. Some of the men from both regiments were exchanging long-range shots at the jeering Russians lining the fort's walls.

At this point Colonel McVeigh began riding

forward through the jumbled ranks, thrashing the men with the flat of his sword and swearing the vilest oaths.

"Damn you to hell, you cowardly scum!" he was yelling. "You'll take the Redan or I'll hang every tenth man of you! And don't think I'll forget your faces, any one of you. Get on, you gutter spawn!"

He had reached the front and was pointing at the Redan with his sword when he was hit and pitched to the ground over his horse's tail. Some of the Fusiliers sent up a cheer but were quickly brought to order by their officers.

In the same instant I saw Tom lowering his rifle from his shoulder as though he had taken slow, deliberate aim at something. He ran forward, across the fire-swept area in front of the enemy fortifications.

"Come on, lads! Let's give it one more go!" I heard him shout.

About twenty of the men followed him. I would have done so, but was pulled up short by Sergeant Major Mulcahy, who grabbed me by the collar.

"Stay where you are, Pope!" he said sharply. "We take our orders from Mr Adair. That's a brave thing those men are doing, but it's pointless and I'll not have you throwing your life away!"

Tom's sudden rush must have taken the Russians by

surprise, for about half of those with him managed to reach the wall. They managed to raise one of the fallen ladders. I saw Tom race up it to fight his way through the defences, then he disappeared from view. The Russians flung down the ladder and the rest of his party were shot down around it in the ditch below.

We were ordered to return to our trenches. We did so sullenly, arguing among ourselves as to why we had failed for a second time at the Redan. The arguments were silenced by a sudden cry of "The French have taken the Malakoff!" I turned and saw that the Tricolour was now flying above the battered fort. We cheered then and we cheered even louder when, an hour or so later, the French turned the Malakoff's guns on the interior of the Redan, making it impossible for the enemy to remain there.

That night the Russians blew up the rest of their forts and burned their ships. They abandoned the city and retreated across the harbour on their bridge of boats, which they also destroyed. Sevastopol was ours. We had set out to destroy the Tsar's great fortress and naval base, and that is what we had done. We felt a great sense of relief that the siege was over, and were grateful that we had survived, but, once again, we had lost too many of our comrades that day to feel like celebrating. I worried what had become of Tom. I also wonder whether he had had a hand in McVeigh's death. I had certainly seen him take deliberate aim at someone – was it at a Russian on the walls of the Redan, or was it at McVeigh?

Next morning a casualty clearing party returned from the Redan. I asked them whether they had come across Tom's body in the ruins and they said they had not. This meant that he was probably alive, but possibly wounded. A little later I caught a snatch of conversation between Major Manningham and Mr Adair and guessed that they were talking about Colonel McVeigh.

"I detested the man, but he was certainly no coward," said Major Manningham.

"How did it happen?" asked Mr Adair.

"Shot twice in the back," replied the Major. "The bullets could have been Russian, fired as he turned to urge the men on. Or..." He shrugged.

"You mean...?"

"Perhaps. He *was* close to the Queen's Fusiliers, many of whom had good cause to wish him dead. Nothing can be proved, and indeed, if anyone on our side did fire the shots they could have been killed in that last attack. Your guess is as good as the next man's."

I came across Paddy, who I hadn't seen since the night before the attack. I told him what I knew about McVeigh's death and my worries about Tom's possible part in it. Paddy had his own way of thinking things through, and although he gave the impression of being happy-go-lucky, he was actually very shrewd.

"Well, now, there's ways o' lookin' at it," he said after a few moments' deep thought. "Ye say the man McVeigh had two bullets in him. They might be Russian and they might be British, or they might be both. Now how will ye know which killed him first, let alone who fired it, with all that was goin' on at the time? 'Tis best ye don't worry yer head about it, for the truth will be hard to come by."

I wasn't altogether convinced by this, but if Tom had fired the fatal shot I couldn't really blame him, for the thousand lashes McVeigh had promised him would certainly have had fatal results, and the chances were that I would have had to administer some of them. I was, however, somehow sure that Tom was alive. A few days later Paddy and I obtained permission to go and look for him among the wounded at the Russian military hospital in Sevastopol, which had not been evacuated when the Russians left. The city still looked handsome from a distance, but it was a ruin. Many of the fine buildings had been burned and stood roofless. Others had collapsed into their cellars because of the bombardment. Even the churches had not been spared. The harbour was full of wrecked or sunken ships. It was truly a place of desolation. Those who had expected to make a fortune from looting were sorely disappointed for the French zouaves had got into the town first and had taken everything that was not nailed down. I saw one of them carrying a huge painting in a gilt frame on his head – what he intended to do with it I have no idea.

We asked for directions to the Russian military hospital. When we got there the sights and smells were horrible. The wounded and dying lay crowded together on the floor. Some British and French doctors and orderlies were doing their best, but the task of caring for so many was beyond them. One of the orderlies told us that the Russians had sent a boat across the harbour with a flag of truce, requesting us to release their wounded. This had been readily agreed to and arrangements for their transport were being made. We asked the orderly whether there were any British wounded in the hospital. He shook his head, saying that they had all been removed to our own hospitals, and that as far as he could remember there were no men from the 110th among them. The thought crossed my mind that if Tom had been lying wounded in the Redan, he might have been blown apart when the French opened fire on the fort.

After we had taken Sevastopol the months passed quietly. The Russians fired at us from time to time across the harbour, and we returned the compliment, but these exchanges were mere annoyances. The Tsar who started this war was now dead and the new Tsar was said to want peace, if terms could be agreed. I was often employed with working parties which, under the direction of the engineers, completed the destruction of the great forts that guarded the harbour entrance, so that they could never be used again. The number of guns we had captured was beyond counting.

When we were not at work there were sporting events held behind the camps. These included race meetings and contests of every kind between regiments and I took up hockey. We had no fear of the coming winter, for we were well clad, comfortably housed and had good rations. I remembered that once we said we would eat our Christmas dinner in

Sevastopol. Well, we did that, although we were a year later than we had expected, and it had cost thousands of lives to get here, mainly from disease. But it was a grand dinner, with turkey and all the trimmings, plum pudding, mince pies and the many good things people at home had sent out to us, and we drank a toast to all our lost comrades whom we wished could be sharing it with us.

Major Manningham was confirmed as commander of the regiment and promoted to lieutenant colonel. Likewise, Mr Adair became a captain. Colonel Manningham was clearly determined to restore the standard of discipline in the regiment and the opportunity arose when we received our back-pay for several months. Some of the newest recruits used it to get drunk, start fights and abuse several NCOs. Colonel Manningham awarded 50 lashes each to three of the worst offenders and I was required to administer some of these. I did not enjoy it, but I had helped to bury better men than them.

The New Year came and went, and little seemed to change, but on 29th February an armistice was declared while the politicians discussed peace terms. In fact, hardly a shot had been fired since December and boredom had become our worst enemy. It was announced that the Queen was to confer a special decoration known as the Victoria Cross upon those officers and men who displayed outstanding bravery during the recent campaign. The Cross was to be made of bronze from cannon we captured in Sevastopol.

On 22nd March there was a parade at which we were handed our campaign medal. The ribbon had clasps recording the battles at which the wearer was present. My own medal had clasps for Alma, Balaklava, Inkerman and Sevastopol. I was uncertain whether Balaklava was deserved as we were only in contact with the enemy during the final stages of the battle, but the rest were honestly earned. The Sultan of Turkey also awarded us a medal.

Shortly after the parade, we exchanged our prisoners for those held by the Russians. About twenty of the regiment's men, taken at Inkerman or the Redan, walked into our camp one day. It was difficult

150

to recognize any of them, for they were wearing fur hats and thick Russian overcoats. One of them walked up to Paddy and me, grinning broadly.

"Hello, Michael, hello, Paddy," he said, shaking our hands warmly. "I'm glad to see you're both still here."

The voice and the eyes were familiar, but I simply could not recognize the bearded man in front of me.

"Faith, I thought it was Tom Wood's ghost I was lookin' at!" exclaimed Paddy in astonishment. "But sure enough, isn't it the man himself, in the flesh!"

"Tom!" I cried. "We had no idea what had happened to you!"

"Well, after I'd got into the Redan I was surrounded, knocked flat and had half a dozen bayonets at my throat," Tom explained. "But a Russian officer stopped them killing me, saying I was a brave fellow and deserved better. I was marched off and they took me with them when they left the city that night. Since then I must have been marched halfway round Russia."

"Did they treat you decently?" I asked.

"By and large, they did. Some of the better sort even invited us into their homes. It was the lesser fry, the jailers and such, who robbed us and kept us without food. However, when the chance came, we complained to the authorities and they did something

151

about it. Those who had abused us got a good hiding from the whips of the Cossack police. You should have seen 'em dance!"

We both laughed, but Tom's face darkened.

"And now I suppose I've got to face Colonel McVeigh and a flogging of my own," he said after a pause.

"No you don't," I said. "McVeigh is dead. He was killed at the Redan."

"Would ye believe it, there's talk that some of our own fellers who didn't care much for him put a couple o' bullets into him!" said Paddy, perhaps hoping to draw him on the subject.

Tom rubbed his beard for a moment, staring into the distance.

"Is that a fact?" he said in his quiet way. "Well then, it seems that all is well with the world – save that I can't wait to get rid of these darned whiskers!"

I suspected that he might have known more than he cared to say, but there was no point in pressing the subject and we let it drop. We would never know for certain who had put an end to McVeigh's evil life.

At the beginning of April we began packing up and getting ready to sail home. Under the terms of the peace agreement we were to hand back Sevastopol, for what it was worth, while the Russians gave guarantees that there would be no more attacks on their Turkish neighbours. Before we left, a grand review of all the Allied armies was held for a Russian general, whose name, I believe, was Luders. There were 300,000 men on parade, British, French, Sardinians and Turks. It took all day for them to pass the stand from which the General took the salute.

July 1856

We arrived back at Thornbury to a welcome none of us will ever forget. The Band had been sent home during that first terrible winter, taking the captured silver drums with them, as there was no point in their remaining in the Crimea. Now, Colonel Manningham had sent instructions ahead of us for them to meet us at the railway station, bringing the drums and our white drummers' coats with them. While we were forming up in the station yard, the town band played "Rule Britannia" and other stirring tunes. The Colours, bullet-riddled and ragged with the honourable scars they received at the Alma, were marched on to parade. The town band fell silent and we were given the order to march, striking up "Ça Ira", a fine rousing French tune. As we emerged from the station gates we were struck by what seemed to be a tidal wave of cheering. It was deafening. Flags were strung across the street and there were more hanging from windows and being waved by dense crowds. "Welcome back, boys!" they were shouting, and "Well done, lads!", and they were calling out the names of men they knew in the ranks. For a brief moment I was saddened by the thought that less than half the men who had marched off to war two years earlier were still with us. Then I saw my family, with my younger brothers and sisters jumping up and down and waving flags for all they were worth. "Michael! Michael! Michael!" they were shouting, "Over here! Over here!" I felt a sudden surge of joy at seeing them all again. I felt on top of the world and smiled hugely at them.

We marched to the Town Hall, where the Corporation and the gentry of the county had subscribed to give us a magnificent dinner of the finest roast beef, washed down with bottle after bottle of beer. There were several speeches, to which Colonel Manningham replied courteously, though I cannot remember what was said for by then we were so full of good cheer that we simply sat grinning at each other. Outside, we formed up again, still full of jollity, but the second we struck up "Here's to the Maiden of Bashful Fifteen" our backs straightened, our heads went up and our chests went out. As we marched into Corunna Barracks the archway echoed the thunder of our drums, a sound which at times I thought I would never hear again.

Our families were allowed into the barracks to see us, and tea was provided for them. There were handshakes and hugs and everyone seemed to be talking at once, asking question after question. My father seemed to be in better spirits than at any time since the death of my mother. He said that now my elder brothers had learned the trade, he had been able to accept more and more business, so that the family was no longer desperately short of money. Tom, who had never mentioned his family, and Paddy, whose family were in Ireland, came over and joined us, so that we became noisier than ever. Then, to my surprise, I was introduced to Miss Mary Cottrell and her parents. Miss Cottrell was indeed very pretty and blushed remarkably pink when my youngest sister remarked, "She would not be left behind when there was a chance of meeting *her* soldier!"

The men sent home earlier from the Crimea because of wounds or sickness told us that while there were still some who were uncomfortable in the presence of soldiers, most had stopped regarding us as blackguards and were even pleased to keep company with us. Perhaps some good has come of it, after all, although I couldn't help thinking that we had paid a terrible price to be accepted.

March 1857

On 15th March I requested and was granted an interview with Colonel Manningham. Since our return to Thornbury, I had been walking out regularly with Mary Cottrell and there was an understanding between us. I retained the fine repeater watch I was given at the Alma, but sold the gold cigar case for a fair price to a jeweller and exchanged the gold roubles for sovereigns at a bank. As my family were happily no longer in need of financial assistance, I invested the money with a penny bank, where it will earn interest and give us a start when we marry. However, the regulations stated that first I must obtain my commanding officer's approval, which Colonel Manningham declined to give for the present.

"Your savings will undoubtedly help you, Pope," he said. "Nevertheless, you cannot support a wife on a drummer's pay, let alone a family. You must remember the old saying that when the wolf comes to the door, love will fly out of the window."

He then said that he was well aware that I was a

good soldier, and that he was promoting me to corporal, although it would mean leaving the Drums and joining one of the companies permanently. I would also become one of the regiment's musketry instructors, because I am a good shot. He said that if I discharged my new duties satisfactorily, he would promote me to sergeant in a year, or two at the most, for although I would be young for the rank I had ample experience and ability. He added that on a sergeant's pay I would be able to provide for a family, and if Mary was the girl for me she would certainly be prepared to wait a little longer. She said that she would and our future seems assured.

As for my old comrades Tom and Paddy, Tom was already well established as a sergeant and is likely to become a sergeant major one day. For saving Captain Manningham's life at Inkerman he had received the Victoria Cross. As to whether or not he had a hand in the death of Colonel McVeigh, we shall never know. Paddy now had a corporal's stripes upon his arm. We had, the three of us, shared good times and bad together and I hope that we shall remain friends for many years to come.

Historical note

Early in 1853 a brawl took place between Greek
Orthodox and Roman Catholic monks at Bethlehem,
during which several Orthodox monks were killed.
Bethlehem then lay under Turkish rule. Tsar Nicholas
I of Russia, who regarded himself as guardian of the
Orthodox faith, decided that he would destroy the
Turkish Empire and invaded the Turkish province of
Romania. However, neither France, which regarded
herself as the champion of Roman Catholic rights in
the Middle East, nor Great Britain, were prepared to
tolerate the expansion of Russian power into the area,
and they decided to support the Sultan of Turkey.

On 4 October 1853 Turkey declared war on Russia.
On land, her troops halted the Russian invasion of
Romania, but on 30 November a small squadron of
her warships was destroyed by the Russian Black Sea
Fleet at Sinope. A Franco-British fleet entered the
Black Sea on 3 January 1854 and on 28 March Great
Britain and France declared war on Russia. Both sent
troops to assist the Turks in Romania, from which the

Russians had already begun withdrawing as a result of diplomatic pressure from the Austrian Empire, which was also opposed to the Tsar's expansionist plans.

The Allies then decided that to punish the Tsar they would destroy the Russian naval base of Sevastopol. They landed at Calamita Bay in the Crimea and defeated a Russian field army at the Battle of the Alma on 20 September. The mounted staff officer referred to by Michael on page 74 really existed. On several occasions during the battle he gave orders to regiments and in some cases they obeyed, causing considerable confusion. His identity has never been traced and it is possible that he was an English-speaking Russian whose task it was to create as much disorder as possible.

If the elderly Allied generals had possessed more drive, the Allies could have entered Sevastopol almost unopposed immediately after the Battle of the Alma. Instead, they chose to march round it and establish a formal siege. This not only allowed the Russians to reinforce the garrison of the city and construct defences, but also to form a new army nearby. On 25 October a Russian attempt to break the siege by capturing the British supply base was foiled at the Battle of Balaklava, during which the famous Charge of the Light Brigade took place. On 5 November the Russian army and the Sevastopol garrison again attempted to break the siege by attacking the British camps, but were repulsed after a hard-fought battle on Mount Inkerman. In this the Russians sustained 11,959 casualties, including 4,400 killed, while the British and French losses were, respectively, 2,573 and 1,743 killed and wounded.

In an era when battles were fought at such murderously close range that soldiers could see every detail of their opponents' uniforms, strict discipline was required to keep men in the firing line. Serious breaches of discipline were punished by flogging.

During the next few months the British supply and medical systems lapsed into chaos. As Michael relates, the troops spent the harsh winter of 1854–5 without adequate shelter, clothing, fuel, rations or medical care, as a result of which thousands of them died from disease and exposure. By the end of January 1855 the British army in the Crimea had only 11,000 men fit for duty, no less than 23,000 men being listed as sick or wounded. The scandal was revealed by the despatches of William Howard Russell, the correspondent of *The Times,* who is mentioned in this story. This marked a turning point in the public's attitude to its soldiers, who had previously been regarded as little better than drunken brutes. The men's bravery and suffering as reported by Russell provoked admiration and sympathy among his readers and the public in general responded generously by donating warm clothing and many other items. Lord Aberdeen's government fell and was replaced by one that quickly reformed the Army's supply and medical services, the latter assisted by Florence Nightingale's nurses in the hospital at Scutari.

In January 1855 the Allies were joined by a Sardinian contingent. The siege of Sevastopol continued and in June some of the Russians' smaller fortifications were taken, although assaults on two important forts, the Malakoff and the Redan, failed with heavy casualties. British and French gunboats were now operating in the Sea of Azov, where they all but destroyed the Russians' supply line, depriving them of ammunition and food.

On 16 August the Russians, now desperate, made a final attempt to break the siege by attacking the French and Sardinians at Traktyr Ridge, but were repulsed. On 8 September the Allies assaulted the Malakoff and the Redan for a second time. The Malakoff was taken and since its guns commanded the interior of the Redan, where the assault had failed again, the latter was evacuated. The Russians abandoned Sevastopol the same night after blowing up their fortifications and burning their warships in the harbour. Under the terms of the peace treaty concluded early the following year, Russia provided guarantees that she would mount no further attacks on the Turkish Empire.

Although the Allied war against Russia was also fought elsewhere, the Crimea was its principal arena and gave its name to the war. A total of 111 Victoria Crosses were awarded to officers and men of the Royal Navy and the British Army for acts of supreme courage during the Crimean War.

Timeline

Spring 1853 Violent disputes between Roman Catholic and Orthodox monks in Bethlehem result in several of the latter being killed. The Russian Tsar makes impossible demands on the Sultan of Turkey, under whose rule Bethlehem lies.

July 1853 Russian troops invade the Turkish province of Romania.

4 October 1853 Turkey declares war on Russia.

30 November 1853 Russian Black Sea Fleet destroys a Turkish squadron at Sinope.

3 January 1854 British and French warships enter the Black Sea.

28 March 1854 Great Britain and France declare war on Russia.

10 May 1854 British and French troops arrive at Varna in Bulgaria.

Summer 1854 Russian troops withdraw from Romania but the Allies decide that the Tsar must be taught a lesson and decide to destroy the Russian naval base of Sevastopol in the Crimea.

13–18 September 1854 Allies land at Calamita Bay in the Crimea.

20 September 1854 Russians defeated at Battle of the Alma.

8 October 1854 Siege of Sevastopol begins.

25 October 1854 Russian attempt to break the siege is defeated at the Battle of Balaklava. (Charge of the Light Brigade takes place.)

5 November 1854 Second Russian attempt to break siege is defeated at Battle of Inkerman. Generals on both sides have little control over what is taking place and it becomes known as "The Soldiers' Battle".

Winter 1854–1855 The British Army's supply and medical services break down, causing terrible suffering among the troops. William Howard Russell's despatches to *The Times* cause public outrage, leading to the fall of the government. Urgent steps taken to remedy the situation.

26 January 1855 Sardinian contingent joins Allies.

24 May 1855 Allies capture Kerch. Commencement of naval operations to sever Russian communications in the Sea of Azov.

7–18 June 1855 Allied assault on Sevastopol. Some of the Russians' outer defences are taken but assaults on the Malakoff and Redan forts fail.

16 August 1855 Final Russian attempt to break the siege is defeated by the French and Sardinians at the Battle of Traktyr Ridge.

8 September 1855 Allied assault on the Redan fails but the Malakoff is taken. Russians withdraw from Sevastopol.

1 February 1856 Preliminary Peace Conference. Virtual ceasefire.

28 February–30 March 1856 Negotiation and signature of Peace Treaty at Congress of Paris. Russia gives guarantees that she will not attack the Turkish Empire again. Allies hand back Sevastopol and sail for home.

Picture acknowledgements

P167	Map of Europe and the Ottoman Empire, András Bereznay
P168	Map of Crimea, András Bereznay
P169	Group from the 41st Regiment outside hut, Crimea 1855, The Royal Archives © Her Majesty Queen Elizabeth II/James Robertson
P170	Minie rifle, Courtesy of the Director, National Army Museum, London
P171	Unloading stores at Balaklava, Courtesy of the Director, National Army Museum, London
P172	Military band playing in camp, Crimea 1855, The Royal Archives © Her Majesty Queen Elizabeth II/James Robertson
P173	Cossacks of the Don region, 1854-5, The Royal Archives © Her Majesty Queen Elizabeth II/Carol Popp de Szathmari
P174	A Lancer on his horse, Mary Evans Picture Library
P175	18th Hussars, Mary Evans Picture Library
P176	Crimean trench position by James Robertson, V & A Picture Library

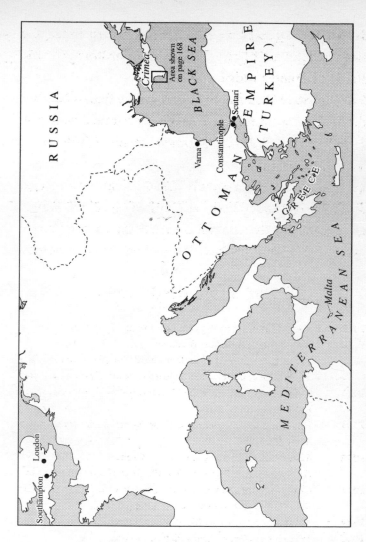

Map showing the location of Crimea and many of the places mentioned in this book.

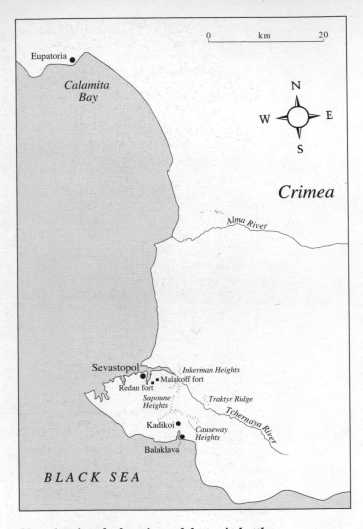

Map showing the locations of the main battles.

A group from the 41st Regiment, including bandsmen and drummers in their white jackets. The huts behind them were built as a result of the public outrage at the conditions of the camps over the 1844-5 winter.

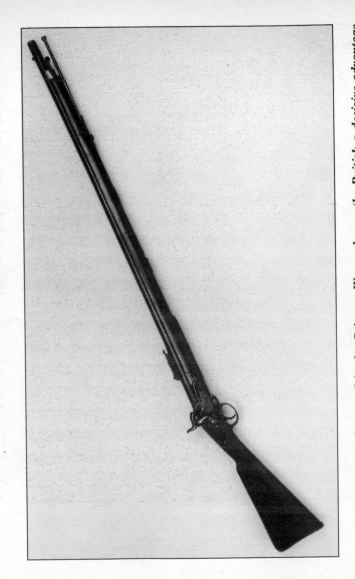

The Minie rifle was first used in the Crimean War and gave the British a decisive advantage against the Russians in many battles.

Unloading provisions at Balaklava harbour. In the foreground are the railway tracks that were laid in 1855 to replace the carrying parties that had taken supplies on foot up to the British camps.

A group of officers, many with their dogs, listening to the bandsmen in their distinctive white jackets playing in a Crimean camp in 1855.

Russian Cossacks from the regiment that faced the Charge of the Light Brigade at Balaklava.

A member of the 17th Lancers, the regiment that led the disastrous Charge of the Light Brigade.

British officers of the 18th Hussars in full dress.

A captured Russian fortification lined with sandbags and wicker baskets filled with earth and stones. Two large guns remain in position.